Other titles in the series

HIKAYAT

SHORT STORIES BY LEBANESE WOMEN

Edited by

Roseanne Saad Khalaf

TELEGRAM

London   San Francisco

British Library Cataloguing-in-Publication Data
A catalogue record for this book is available from the British Library

ISBN 10: 1-84659-011-6
ISBN 13: 978-1-84659-011-5

F146.422
€15·00

copyright © Roseanne Khalaf, 2006
Copyright for individual stories rests with the authors and translators

This edition published 2006 by Telegram Books

Manufactured in Lebanon

TELEGRAM
26 Westbourne Grove, London W2 5RH
825 Page Street, Suite 203, Berkeley, California 94710
www.telegrambooks.com

Contents

Acknowledgments

'Chat' is from *The Stranger's Letters*; 'Improvisations on a Missing String' is from the novel of the same name; 'The Language of the Secret' is from the novel of the same name; 'The Story of Warda' is from the novel *B for a House Named Beirut*; 'A Slice of Beach' is from the novel of the same name; 'A Pomegranate Notebook' is from the novel of the same name; and 'Khamsin' is from the novel of the same name.

Special thanks are due to translators Catherine Cobham and Denys Johnson-Davies, who graciously provided translations for this collection.

Introduction

The selections presented in this anthology bring together contemporary stories and prose pieces by established Lebanese women authors as well as promising young writers. They highlight the diversity, startling originality and compelling richness of women's voices and experiences in a dynamic, fast-changing cosmopolitan society. Collectively, the narratives span three distinct but overlapping eras: the pre-war period, often considered the golden age in Lebanon; the two decades of protracted civil strife; followed by the postwar phase of reconstruction and reconciliation.

During the late 1950s, a group of talented women writers appeared on the Lebanese literary scene. Before this time, the contributions of women were few and the Lebanese canon, such as it was, consisted almost exclusively of works written by men. In an unexpected move, and in contrast to the dynamic of previous generations, these authors expertly relocated their prose to a more central position. Now, for the first time, women writers were competing with men in literary and commercial arenas. Together they mapped an entirely different landscape, writing in ways that radically redefined traditional literary expectations. To a large extent, their emerging influence is attributed to innovative themes and styles, coupled with an unthreatening approach. In a bid to address relevant issues, they wrote gender-informed narratives about identity and desire, defying the conventions imposed on women by a restrictive society. Female protagonists were boldly empowered to voice their own needs and expectations in hitherto unheard of ways, adamantly rejecting previously acceptable themes that reduced them to nothing more than objects of the male gaze. Interestingly, their narratives correspond to the last two phases of Elaine Showalter's three-stage Gynocriticism theory of female literary evolution in the Western novel (1977): the feminist stage of protest against traditional standards (1880–1920) and the female stage of searching for a new identity (1920 onwards).[1]

By choosing a reflexive approach, women novelists could now rely almost entirely on topics drawn from personal experience. More importantly, however, their stance, whether intentional or accidental, served an immediate purpose: it ensured quick entry into the canon from which they had previously been excluded. Perhaps in writing differently they posed no direct threat to the male literary establishment, but whatever the reasons the results, so soon realised, had immediate and far-reaching consequences. Apart from their creativity often exceeding and overshadowing works written by men,[2] their texts successfully moved female fiction out of the margins and into the mainstream. For the first time, prose that voiced gendered rebellion was redefining the way women wrote and having a decisive impact in shaping the imaginative work that followed. Their fiction stood in stark contrast with that of the previous generation of women authors who had so readily imitated established male literary traditions

1. Showalter, Elaine, *A Literature of Their Own* (Princeton 1977), p.13.
2. Agacy, Samira, 'Lebanese Women's Fiction: Urban Identity and the Tyranny of the Past', *International Journal of Middle East Studies* 33 (2001), p. 503,

and who fit easily into Showalter's first phase, the imitation of the dominant literary tradition (1840–80).

Layla Baalbaki, Rima Alamuddin and Emily Nasrallah are three compelling examples of writers who became distinguished for their remarkable literary activity during the pre-war period. All came from radically different backgrounds and confessional groups but together they created means of self-expression that dramatically altered the way Lebanese woman crafted their prose. Layla Baalbaki gained instant notoriety for her outspokenness, especially against sexual segregation in Arab society. In fact, the publication of her collection in 1964, *Safinat Hanan ila al-Qamar* (*Spaceship of Tenderness to the Moon*), led to her being unsuccessfully persecuted by the Lebanese authorities who deemed her writing too sexually explicit and therefore capable of corrupting public morality, particularly among the young.

In seeking to transform the lives of women, her candid prose boldly and critically challenges the prejudiced values and accepted attitudes so deeply ingrained in a rigid patriarchal system. Her defiance of gender inequalities scrutinises the sacred institutions of marriage and motherhood, forcing even the male characters in her texts to rethink and question blind conformity. Clearly, her considerable impact was not limited to Lebanon. Zeidan claims that Baalbaki was much admired in literary circles throughout the Arab world and credits her with 'bringing the discourse of a female point of view into the mainstream of Arab writing'.[1] Until then, literature, emblematic of a patriarchal culture, was written from distinctly male points of view. Moreover, Baalbaki was the first Arab woman writer to employ first-person narration in fiction, using the pronoun 'I' to stress the identity and individuality of the

---

1. Zeidan, Joseph, *Arab Women Novelists: The Formative Years and Beyond* (New York 1995), p. 139.

female protagonist.[1] With her novel *Ana Ahya* (*I Survive*, 1958), she ushered in a whole new era in women's fiction, highlighting issues of personal freedom, autonomy and self-fulfilment that influenced the 'agenda' of later novels.[2] Undoubtedly, Baalbaki's accomplishments paved the way for writers in the generations to come.

In 1960, at the age of nineteen, Rima Alamuddin wrote her first novel, *Spring to Summer,* and after graduating from the American University of Beirut she studied English Literature at Girton College, Cambridge. 'The Cellist' which appeared in her collection, *The Sun is Silent*, was published in 1964, a year after her untimely death. It reveals the fiercely independent mind of a professional woman whose identity and self-worth exist entirely outside the male gaze.

Emily Nasrallah's first novel, *Tuyur Aylul* (*Birds of September*, 1962), explored what later became a common theme in her work: the alienation of the younger generation from the restrictive and stifling conventions of village life and their determination to break away in search of more promising opportunities. Many moved to cities, thereby compounding the expansion of urbanisation, whereas even larger numbers emigrated, thus exacerbating the country's proverbial 'brain drain'. In subsequent years, with the onset of the Lebanese civil war, the tragedy and devastation it inflicted on the country and its people became a backdrop to many of her most poignant stories. 'The Green Bird', taken from her collection *A House Not Her Own: Stories From Beirut* (1992), tells of a grief-stricken man's obsessive belief in the power of miracles to reverse his pain and ease the shock of his son's violent death. In relating this heart-rending tale, the narrator stoically gains strength to endure the incomprehensible horrors of war.

With the outbreak of the Lebanese War in 1975, which

1. Ibid, p. 99.
2. Ibid, p. 155.

spanned nearly two decades, came a surge of literary creativity. While the previous generation was essentially concerned with matters of personal identity and the desire for individual freedom and self-expression, the focus now shifted, primarily during the first half of the war (up to the 1982 Israeli invasion) to confront a much darker reality. During this time, as women writers became increasingly consumed by Lebanon's tragedy, they shifted their narrative gaze away from the brutal fighting to concentrate instead on the traumas resulting from protracted and random violence. While it is easy to attribute their stance to lack of military knowledge, it was more likely an attempt to gain distance from the atrocities of warfare in order to explore deeper concerns.

Regardless of the reasons, their prose provided graphic glimpses into the tragic human consequences of violence by delving into the terrain of pain, fear and despair that paralysed the daily lives of an entire civilian population and transformed the war-torn nation into a living hell. As their fiction demonstrates, opposition to the war, alongside the exploration of alternatives to violence as a means of resolving conflict, became recurring and increasingly dominant themes. The effect was startling. Silent, marginal voices capable of destabilizing and challenging the master war narrative could now be heard in the wider public sphere.

The women who wrote during the war, or the 'Beirut Decentrists' as Cooke names them, 'shared Beirut as their home and war as their experience'.[1] They were able to transcend confessional and political loyalties in order to concentrate almost entirely on the omitted stories of pain and suffering. Hence they carved out a discursive space of particular significance, one that contributed a crucial and hitherto overlooked dimension to the Lebanese literary canon.

At the same time, in their war-telling, literary figures such

1. Cooke, Mariam, *War's Other Voices: Women Writers on the Lebanese Civil War* (Cambridge 1988), p. 3.

as Etel Adnan, Hanan al-Shaykh, Emily Nasrallah, Hoda Barakat and Nazik Saba Yared moved beyond simply exposing or recording daily atrocities to produce oppositional discourses and alternative visions that redefined nationalism. Their humane approach, encouraging non-violent means of bringing the war to an end, created a narrative of peace politics.[1]

Cooke's views have not gone unchallenged. Some scholars[2] have contested her designation of the Beirut Decentrists by drawing a clear division between women writers who emigrated, thus becoming Francophone or Anglophone expatriates, emigrants or exiles, and those who remained 'under the bombs in Beirut'.[3] Indeed, Hoda Barakat, Najwa Barakat, Hanan al-Shaykh, Mai Ghoussoub and Etel Adnan are among those who settled abroad, becoming exiled decentrists residing in Western cities. Distance enabled them to write 'from the vantage point of informed outsiders looking in, and more specifically, looking back'.[4] Consequently, they reclaimed the war experience with 'the geographical and temporal distance necessary for an adequate assessment of the war's personal and communal implications.' In the case of Etel Adnan, movement between numerous worlds (Beirut, London and California) and multiple cultures creates a new ethos for understanding subjectivity. As a 'trans-national writer', her awareness takes her 'to a space beyond the dogma of nationalism and other codified aspects of subjectivity as gender and race.'[5]

---

1. *Mapping Peace 1999*: edited by Shehadi.
2. Amyuni, Mona Takieddine, 'A Panorama of Lebanese Women Writers, 1975–1995', in Lamia Rustum Shehadeh's *Women Writers on the Lebanese Civil War* (Florida 1999).
3. Amyuni, p. 9.
4. Fadda-Conrey, Carol, 'Exilic Memories of War: Lebanese Women Writers Looking Back', *Arabasque: Arabic Literature in Translation and Arab Diasporic Writing*, special issue of *Studies in the Humanities 30* (2003), p. 8.
5. Shoaib, Mahwash, 'Surpassing Borders and Folded Maps: Etel Adnan's

Among the writers represented in this collection, Etel Adnan and Hanan al-Shaykh are, arguably, two of the most prominent and widely read. Adnan's richly detailed story, 'The Power of Death' is a mesmerising tale of friendship that depicts an embittered man whose life has gone horribly wrong. Throughout, he is haunted by an irreversible decision taken in his youth. Hanan al-Shayk is perhaps best known for her novel, *Hikayat Zahra* (*The Story of Zahra*, 1980), a skilfully wrought work that offers a scathing feminist commentary on life during the Lebanese war. In contrast, 'The Hot Seat', a compact and blunt tale, exists completely outside the war experience. Seemingly innocent daydreams quickly end in an abrupt and startling reversal. In the excerpt from Nazik Saba Yared's novel, *Improvisations on a Missing String*, Saada is saddened by her sister's decision to leave Lebanon, while the selection from Alawiya Sobh's novel, *Stories by Mariam*, depicts a young woman's earnest account of thwarted romantic love and disappointment across the religious and social divide. It raises disturbing questions about the moral dilemmas of liberated women living in a society with rigidly defined rules. Finally, the extract from *B for a House Named Beirut* by Iman Humaydan Younes tells the story of Warda's desperate attempt to locate her daughter whom she imagines has been kidnapped.

With the Taif Accord in 1990, the Lebanese war was officially brought to a close, yet the lingering horrors along with the need to reconstruct and address the inevitable consequences, continue to inform women's prose. In fact, much of the fiction produced in the postwar period is concerned with sorting out the past, which may inevitably be a way of clearing ground for the literature of the future. Writers revisit a landscape haunted by pain, cruelty and retribution, challenging the conspiracy of silence or collective

Location is There', *Arabasque: Arabic Literature in Translation and Arab Diasporic Writing*, p. 23.

amnesia that characterises the attitude of many Lebanese. The past in their narratives is intricately linked to the present, often rendering stories more unsettling than enjoyable.

Mishka Moujabbar Mourani's 'The Fragrant Garden' exposes the seemingly tolerant façade of Lebanese postwar society. Ironically, the husband fondly remembers what in hindsight he describes as idyllic war routines while candidly admitting his resentment of the returnees who are invading his space. 'The Phone Call' from Renée Hayek's collection *Portraits of Forgetfulness* (1994) is the story of a dysfunctional woman whose empty life is a result of the numbing experience of war. Throughout, the protagonist is trapped in the heavy stillness of Hayek's prose. In Merriam Haffar's 'Pieces of a Past Life' Soumaya's genuine grief and concern for her disturbed father, another war victim, is as tender as it is distressing. Haffar, who is herself too young to remember the war, writes to imagine and reconstruct a traumatic moment in the history of her country and to expose the war's debilitating consequences on the life of a family. In Jana Faour's story, 'Not Today' a young woman looks back on a simple but disillusioning childhood episode that strengthens her resolve to transcend the pervasive hostility and ignorance resulting from religious difference.

What differentiates the next group of postwar women writers is the ability to produce storylines that repeatedly decentre romantic as well as rebellious narratives. An unsentimental and deterministic outlook calls for re-imagining and reshuffling themes as well as applying jarring techniques that disturb the rhythm and flow of the prose. In addition, the loosening or dissolution of human bonds, sexual relationships and emotional dilemmas is clearly evident. All these authors craft narratives with liberating and transforming possibilities, each writing against the grain, using innovative wordplay to experiment with form and content.

Mai Ghoussoub's 'Red Lips' and Nadine Touma's 'Red Car' are startlingly original, with vividly rendered settings. In order to reshape mainstream notions of sex, intimacy and love, the stories challenge what normally passes for acceptable behaviour. The language is dark, luxurious, dazzling, with themes that focus on the odd, the edgy, the risky and the peculiar. The prose runs freely, breaking down barriers, conjuring up playful but dangerous fantasy worlds of desire. Moreover, within these surreal arenas, shamelessly uninhibited characters engage in forbidden sexual acts in the most sacred of places: a convent and a mosque. Ghoussoub shakes up the normal flow of the linear text as she juxtaposes and experiments with assertions and insertions. Touma's images, on the other hand, travel through the tale in rapid succession with new meanings attaching to them on the way. Both texts are tightly wrought and dramatically compelling in their desire to transform. They suggest daring possibilities capable of reshaping and radically altering inflexible and essentialist views. 'Omega: Definitions' by Zeina B Ghandour, is relentless in its abrasive immediacy. Direct, snappy and defiant in tone, its power lies in the potential to provoke. The excerpt from Huda Karim's candid novel, *Tranche de plage* ('A Slice of Beach'), transports the reader to the intimacy of two male lovers living in the midst of an unwelcoming culture. Whereas in the selection from Najwa Barakat's gripping thriller, *The Language of the Secret*, the reader is witness to Khaldoun's wild and fanciful secret religious mission.

Stories that break the silence by focusing on what remains unsaid or purposefully ignored offer the possibility of actualizing or realizing change. May Menassa, Jocelyn Awad, Zalfa Feghali, Nada Ramadan, Evelyn Shakir and Patricia Sarrafian Ward all portray female protagonists who defy their domestic and familial situations in varying degrees and with entirely different outcomes. Selections from Menassa's *The Pomegranate Notebook* and Awad's *Khamsin* describe dramatic events: a birth and a marriage, prompting the reader to view the patterns of families over generations. But the real purpose is to expose the rough customs and abuse that rural women are often subjected to. Zalfa Feghali's story, 'Wild Child' is a chilling account of living with the bitter pain of exclusion, drug addiction and, ultimately, madness. From the outset, it is powerfully imagined, heavy with irony and emotionally charged as Nour, the isolated, rebellious protagonist, 'others' the hostile relatives who have so insensitively marginalized her. Nada Ramadan's vignette 'Chores' possesses an air of immediacy while employing a flauntingly feminine style that voices the protagonist's protests along with her desire to be liberated from tedious, confining domestic routines. Because the prose never gives way to emotionalism, the story succeeds in being more than just a vehicle for the dramatisation of wronged womanhood. Hoda Barakat is the acclaimed author of an intensely evocative novel, *The Stone of Laughter* (1990). 'Chat', taken from her recent collection of reflective essays, deplores the callous attitude of Lebanese youth living abroad to the Arabic language.

Evelyn Shakir's 'Name-calling' and Patricia Sarrafian Ward's 'Voice' also provide vividly critical glimpses that give voice to the silence in Lebanese households. Their protagonists share the initial experience of being silenced but ultimately refuse to adopt the silence as their own. Yet finding a voice is not simple, for it requires a series of delicately complex mediations. Shakir's story explores negative aspects of Lebanese culture in the United States and its debilitating consequences on the lives of women. If at first, Dolores lacks the resourcefulness necessary to gain any semblance of independence, she later gains the inner strength to exert her will and restore a sense of self and personal autonomy independent of her role as wife or mother. In 'Voice', Ward crafts a linear tale that is deceptively simple and straightforward due to skilful omissions. When the mysteriously silent girl suddenly appears, the reader wonders what thoughts fill her mind. Then, as the story unfolds, our focus shifts to question her seemingly well-intended employer. The girl, whose shy, vulnerable manner is misleading, presents him with possibilities at once tempting and anxiety-inducing for they awaken suppressed yearnings carefully concealed beneath a thin veneer of respectability. Ironically, the reversal casts doubt on whether the girl ever actually feared her employer.

Shakr and Ward address questions of power and powerlessness, so vital to those who have remained invisible in their culture. By breaking the silence, such stories cleverly disrupt the discourse of the good or obedient woman, exposing situations that raise serious issues pertaining to marriage, generation and culture.

In the last ten years, a group of aspiring young fiction writers has emerged. Not surprisingly, a significant number are hybrid and multicultural returnees, border-crossers who have experienced a high rate of mobility as a result of growing up during the dangerous war years. Their introspective prose is entirely devoid of any youthful optimism, and themes are drawn from the risks, unexpected detours, and intense moments that define their broad experiences and journeys. They share a new post-modern sensibility, assuming a self-critical and cynical outlook that rejects cultural or national identity. Instead the negotiation of multiple identities in shifting contexts assumes particular significance, empowering these writers with rare insight into the reality of cross-cultural situations. The constant repositioning of a self that is hybrid, multiple and continually undergoing change has resulted in distinctly different storytelling, the impact of which could prove groundbreaking in a country that is perhaps on the threshold of a new era.

Hala Alyan's 'Painted Reflections' and Lina Mounzer's 'The

One-eyed Man' reveal the dilemma of being caught between two or more worlds. They explore the difficulties and tensions resulting from diaspora and feelings of displacement associated with simultaneously belonging everywhere and nowhere. These authors base their work on intimate personal experiences, writing stories that are somewhat peculiar and loosely plotted, fluid, non-linear and fragmented. But when read within a specific context, they reflect important aspects of their lives: the tales are a testimony to the uncertainties and instabilities witnessed before and in the aftermath of Prime Minister Rafik Hariri's brutal assassination on 14 February 2005. The Cedar Revolution that followed ended Syria's thirty-year hegemony over Lebanon and was largely instigated and sustained by youthful groups. As might be expected, the collective enthusiasm generated by the uprising did not materialise in the progressive transformations so keenly anticipated by the participants. Consequently, a growing number of returnee writers seem legitimately overwhelmed by a demoralising dissonance between hoped for expectations on the one hand and existing realities on the other. At present, these are the areas being explored by young women writers who refuse to comply with an aborted national consciousness and who continue to question and to expose.

'The One-eyed Man' by Lina Mounzer is about people woven together in a destructive web of kinship and misunderstanding. Ali, the exiled and alienated protagonist, is consumed with scathing bitterness of self, family and nation as he struggles to come to terms with war-related feelings of loss. The unfolding transformation of his character, through fragments and flashbacks, ultimately assumes more importance than his reporting of experience. In Alyan's 'Painted Reflections', a Lebanese American woman embarks on a journey of rediscovery to her homeland, in part to escape the pain of her loss on 9/11, coupled with a desire to experience the left-behind place she has come to know only vicariously through the words or silences of her Lebanese mother. Shortly after her arrival, she witnesses the horrific carnage of Rafik Hariri's assassination. Her response is to embark on an orgy of drugs and alcohol while engaging in a hypnotic frenzy of painting. The destructive intensity with which she confronts the dilemma of being positioned on the crossroads between two cultures, yet unable to draw strength or identity from either, is a recipe for disaster. F146.422

Young returnees like Alyan and Mounzer who have spent their lives dipping in and out of Lebanon during and after the war years possess a remarkably rich consciousness. By weaving stories against more than one landscape, the condition of living between worlds is made critically clear. Constructing layers of narratives, one upon the other and one beside the other, creates spaces of tension and uncertainty between the authors, their protagonists and the multiple societies they inhabit, thus instigating a global, post-modern conversation across time and space. In this way, seemingly personal and private texts are capable of revealing a much wider and ever-expanding story.

Making selections for an anthology is never an easy process, and no single collection can be considered definitive or exhaustive. Inevitably, there will be omissions, sometimes resulting from the delicate issue of 'translatability'. Tales that may be fascinating to read in one language are often problematic in translation. For example, the common practice in Arabic of identifying characters generically as 'the woman' and 'the man' can prove awkward in an English text. The narratives compiled here are translated from Arabic or French unless, of course, they were originally written in English and the inclusion of novel excerpts results from the fact that most Lebanese authors prefer the novel genre to that of the short story. In an attempt to simplify, I have not applied any of the international transliteration systems such as the one used by The Encyclopaedia of Islam or the International Journal of Middle East Studies (IJMAS). Nor has my aim been merely to present a diverse set of stories: because of my commitment to the future, I have attempted to bring together pieces by students as well as the work of authors with already established reputations.

Much of my time since I launched Creative Writing at the American University of Beirut is dedicated to working with aspiring young writers. Throughout the years, it has been immensely rewarding to witness how they shape and are shaped by the stories they tell. Their relentless search for meaning and identity has helped me to better understand the complex, rapidly changing circumstances that constitute their extraordinary reality in an unstable postwar setting. Together we have shared, in varying degrees, disillusionment and hope for a country we so deeply care about. The dreams and aspirations they carefully tuck in their texts fuel my confidence in their ability to become agents of change through the power of imagination and by assuming new direction that will inevitably restructure the future Lebanese literary canon. Precisely for these reasons, we must listen to their storytelling. I have included five of my gifted women students among the contributors – Hala Alyan, Jana Faour, Merriam Haffar, Zelfa Feghali and Lina Mounzer. The reader may wish to keep in mind that their pieces were originally written for our Creative Writing workshops and, as such, belong to the earliest stage of their careers.

Finally, in the gathering and grouping of stories, this anthology also tells its own story of how contemporary Lebanese women continually venture into little-known territory, of how their prose explores and probes the fast-changing and complex terrain of experience, breaking up existing narrative patterns and speaking through the silence. Undoubtedly, their distinguished accomplishments will be a source of creative inspiration for talented new voices in a country in dire need of innovative alternatives.

Roseanne Saad Khalaf

Glossary

Agibeh!	a curiosity of nature
al hamdullah!	Thank God
bulgur	dried, cooked and coarsely ground wheat
dayé	midwife
Khalte	my aunt
Kishk	porridge made of dried yogurt
mansef	a dish of lamb and rice
Rabbi	my God
Tabbouleh	a salad made with parsley, tomatoes, onions and burgul
Teta	grandmother
Ya Berri!	Druze expression meaning 'Oh Creator!'
Yallah	hurry up

LAYLA BAALBAKI

A Spaceship of Tenderness to the Moon

When I closed my eyes I was able to see everything around me, the long settee which fills one vast wall of the room from corner to corner; the shelves on the remaining walls; the small table; the coloured cushions on the carpet; the white lamp, in the shape of a large kerosene one, that dangled from a hole in the wall and rested on the tiled floor. Even the windows we had left curtainless. In the second room was a wide sofa; a table supporting a mirror; a wall-cupboard; and two chairs upholstered in velvet. Since our marriage we hadn't changed a thing in the little house, and I refused to remove anything from it.

I opened my eyelids a little as I heard my husband mumble, 'It's light and we alone are awake in the city.' I saw him rising up in front of the window as the silver light of dawn spread over his face and naked body. I love his naked body.

Once again I closed my eyes: I was able to see every little bit of him, every minute hidden detail, his soft hair, his forehead, nose, chin, the veins of his neck, the hair on his chest, his stomach, his feet, his nails. I called to him to come back and stretch out beside me, that I wanted to kiss him. He didn't move and I knew, from the way he had withdrawn from me and stood far off, that he was preparing himself to say something important. In this sort of situation he can become cruel and stubborn, capable of taking and carrying through decisions. I am the exact opposite: in order to talk things over with him I must take hold of his hand or touch his clothes. So I opened my eyes, threw aside the cushion I was hugging and seized hold of his shirt, spreading it across my chest. Fixing my gaze on the ceiling I asked him if he saw the sea.

'I see the sea,' he answered.

I asked him what colour it was.

'Dark blue on one side,' he said, 'and on the other, a greyish white.'

I asked him if the cypress trees were still there.

'They are still there among the houses that cling close together,' he answered, 'and there's water lying on the roofs of the buildings.'

I said I loved the solitary date-palm, which looked, from where we were, as though it had been planted in the sea and that the cypress trees made me think of white cemeteries.

For a long while he was silent and I remained staring up at the ceiling. Then he said, 'The cocks are calling,' and I quickly told him I didn't like chickens because they couldn't fly and that when I was a child I used to carry them up to the roof of our home and throw them out into space in an attempt to teach them to fly, and both cocks and hens would always land in a motionless heap on the ground.

Again he was silent for a while, then he said that he saw a light come on in the window of a building opposite. I said that even so we were still the only two people awake in the city, the only two who had spent the night entwined in each other's arms. He said that he had drunk too much last night. I quickly interrupted him by saying I hated that phrase 'I drank too much' as though he regretted the yearning frenzy with which he had made love to me. Sensing that I was beginning to get annoyed he changed the subject, saying: 'The city looks like a mound of sparkling precious stones of all colours and sizes.'

I answered that I now imagined the city as coloured cardboard boxes which would fall down if you blew on them: our house alone, with its two rooms, was suspended from a cloud and rode in space. He said that his mouth was dry and he wanted an orange. I finished what I had been saying by stating that although I had never lived in any other city, I hated this one and that had I not dreamt that I would one day meet a man who would take me far, far away from it I would have died of dejection long, long ago. Pretending that he had not heard my last remark he repeated: 'I want an orange, my throat's dry.' I disregarded his request and went on to say that with him I paid no heed to where I was: the earth with its trees, its mountains, rivers, animals and human beings just vanished. Unable to wait further, he burst out at me: 'Why do you refuse to have children?'

I was sad, my heart was wrung, the tears welled up into my eyes, but I didn't open my mouth.

'How long is it since we married?' he asked. I didn't utter a word as I followed him round with my eyes. He stiffened and went on: 'It's a year and several months since we married and you've been refusing and refusing, though you were crazy about children before we married, you were dying for them.'

He swerved and struck the settee with his hands as he burst out: 'Hey chair, don't you remember her entreaties? And you lamp, didn't you hear her wailing? And you cushions, didn't she make you into tiny bodies that she hugged to herself and snuggled up with as she slept? Speak, you inanimate things, speak! Give back to her the words which are buried in you!'

Quietly I said that inanimate things don't feel, don't talk, don't move. Angrily he inquired: 'How do you know they're dead?' I replied that things weren't dead, but that they drew their pulse beats from people. He interrupted me by saying that he wouldn't argue about things now and wouldn't allow me to escape solving the problem as I always did. Absent-mindedly, I explained to him that the things around me, these very things - this settee, this carpet, this wall, this lamp, this vase, the shelves and the ceiling are all a vast mirror that for me reflects the outside world: the houses, the sea, the trees, the sky, the sun, the stars and the clouds. In them I see my past with him, the hours of misery and dejection, the moments of meeting and of tenderness, of bliss and of happiness, and from them I now deduce the shapes of the days to come. I would not give them up.

He became angry and shouted: 'We're back again with things. I want to understand here and now why you refuse to have children!' No longer able to bear it, I shouted that he too at one time refused to have them. He was silent for a while, then he said: 'I refused before we were married, when it would have been foolish to have had one.' Sarcastically I told him that he was afraid of them, those others, those buffoons in the city. He used to beg for their assent, their blessing, their agreement, so that he might see me and I him, so that he might embrace me and I him, so that we might each drown the other in our love. They used to determine our meeting-places, the number of steps to be taken to get there, the time, how much we could raise our voices, the number of breaths we took. And I would watch them as they secretly scoffed at us, shamelessly slept with the bodies they loved, ate three meals a day, smoked cigarettes with cups of coffee and carafes of arak, and guffawed as they vulgarly chewed over stories about us and thought up patterns of behaviour for us to follow the next day. His voice was choked as he mumbled, 'I don't pay attention to others. I was tied to another woman.'

Ah, how can I bear all this torture, all this passionate love for him? He used to be incapable of confessing the bitter truth to her, that he didn't love her, wouldn't love her. Choking, he said that it wasn't easy, he wasn't callous enough to be able to stare into another human being's face and say to her, after nine years of getting up each and every day and finding her there, 'Now the show's over', and turn his back and walk off. I told him to look at my right hand and asked him if my blood was still dripping from it hot on to the floor. 'You were mad,' he mumbled, 'mad when you carried out the idea. I opened this door, entered this room and saw you stretched out on this settee, the veins of your hand slashed, your fingers trailing in a sea of blood. You were mad. I might have lost you.' I smiled sadly as I pulled the shirt up to my chest, my face breathing in its smell. I said that my part in the play required that I should take myself off at the end, and the exit possible for me, the exit I could accept and bear, was a quick death rather than a slow, cruel crawling, like that of the turtle in the film *Mondo Cane* that lost its way in the sands, held in the sun's disc as it searched for the river bank. He repeated sadly that he didn't know I was serious about him. I asked him sarcastically whether he was waiting for me to kill myself in order to be sure that I was telling the truth. I told him that I had lost myself in my love for him: oblivious to all else, I slipped unseen, like a gust of wind, through people's fingers, scorching their faces as I passed through the street. All I was conscious of was the weight of bodies, the height of buildings and his hands. I asked him to draw closer and give me his hand which I longed to hold. He remained standing far off, inflexible, and at once accused me that after all that misery and triumph I was refusing to become pregnant by him, had refused again and again and again, and that from my refusal he understood I no longer loved him.

What? I cried out that he could never accuse me of that. Only yesterday I was stretched out beside him and he gave himself up to deep sleep while I was open-eyed, rubbing my cheeks against his chin, kissing his chest, snuggling up under his arm, searching in vain for sleep. I told him frankly that I was upset by how quickly he got to sleep, and by my being left alone and awake at his side. He quickly denied this, saying that he had never been aware of my being awake. He believed that I dozed off the moment he did. I revealed maliciously that it wasn't the first time he had left me alone. I then related in full yesterday's incident, how he had been asleep breathing quietly, with me stretched close up against him smoking a cigarette, when suddenly in the emptiness of the room through the smoke, I had seen a foot escaping from under the sheets. I moved my own but it didn't move and a shiver ran through the whole of my body. I moved it but it didn't move. I thought of shouting. I hurriedly hid my face in his hair. I was afraid. He moved and the foot moved. I cried silently. I had imagined, had felt, had been unable to tell the difference between his foot and mine. In a faint voice he said, 'In this age people don't die of love.' Quickly seizing the opportunity I said that in this age people didn't beget children. In olden times they knew where the child would be born, who it would be likely to resemble, whether it would be male or female. They would knit it woollen vests and socks, would embroider the hems, pockets and collars of its dresses with coloured birds and flowers. They would amass presents of gold crucifixes for it and medallions with 'Allah bless him', opened palms studded with blue stones and pendants with its name engraved on them. They would reserve a midwife for it, would fix the day of the delivery, and the child would launch out from the darkness and be flung into the light at precisely the estimated time. They would register a piece of land in the child's name, would rent it a house, choose companions for it, decide which school it would be sent to, the profession it would study for, the person it could love and to whom it could bind its destiny. That was a long, long time ago, in the time of your father and my father. He asked: 'Do you believe that twenty years ago was such an age away? What has changed since? What has changed? Can't you and I provide everything that is required for a child?' To soften the blow I explained that before I married I was like a child that lies down on its back in front of the window, gazes up at the stars and stretches out its tiny arm in a desire to pluck them. I used to amuse myself with this dream, with this impossibility, would cling to it and wish it would happen. He asked me: 'Then you were deceiving me?'

Discovering he had changed the conversation into an attack on me so as to win the battle, I quickly told him that only the woman who is unfulfilled with her man eagerly demands a child so that she can withdraw, enjoy being with her child and so be freed. He quickly interrupted me: 'And were you unsatisfied?' I answered him that we had been afraid, had not travelled to the last sweet unexplored regions of experience: we had trembled in terror, had continually come up against the faces of others and listened to their voices. For his sake, for my own, I had defied death in order to live. He was wrong, wrong, to doubt my being madly in love with him.

'I'm at a loss. I don't understand you,' he muttered. I attacked him by saying that was just it. That he also wouldn't understand me if I told him I didn't dare become pregnant, that I would not perpetrate such a mistake.

'Mistake!' he shrieked. 'Mistake!' I clung closer to his shirt, deriving strength from it, and slowly, in a low voice, I told him how scared I was about the fate of any child we might cast into this world. How could I imagine a child of mine, a being nourished on my blood, embraced within my entrails, sharing my breathing, the pulsations of my heart and my daily food, a being to whom I give my features and the earth, how can I bear the thought that in the future he will leave me and go off in a rocket to settle on the moon? And who knows whether or not he'll be happy there? I imagine my child with white ribbons, his fresh face flushed: I imagine him strapped to a chair inside a glass ball fixed to the top of a long shaft of khaki-coloured metal ending in folds resembling the skirt of my Charleston dress. He presses the button, a cloud of dust rises up and an arrow hurls itself into space. No, I can't face it. I can't face it.

He was silent a long, long time while the light of dawn crept in past his face to the corners of the room, his face absent-minded and searching in the sky for an arrow and a child's face. The vein between his eyebrows was knotted: perplexity and strain showed in his mouth. I, too, remained silent and closed my eyes.

When he was near me, standing like a massive tower at a rocket-firing station, my heart throbbed and I muttered to him that I adored his naked body. When he puts on his clothes, especially when he ties his tie, I feel he's some stranger come to pay a visit to the head of the house. He opened his arms and leaned over me. I rushed into his embrace, mumbling crazily, 'I love you, I love you, I love you, I love you, I love you!' He whispered into my hair, 'You're my pearl!' Then he spread the palm of his hand over my lips, drawing me to him with the other hand, and ordered: 'Let us take off, you and I, for the moon.'

Translated by Denys Johnson-Davies

The Cellist

Down the corridor the clock struck three with metallic melancholy. He blew on his fingers, took a spotless handkerchief out of his pocket and ran it lightly over the yellowed keyboard. It was dark in the empty assembly hall, with its neat, cramped rows of wooden benches, its small platform covered with a Gaza rug and high, bare yellow walls.

He jumped down from the platform, ran to the door and tried all the light switches for the fifth time, but there was still no electricity. As he walked back along the platform, up the single wooden step towards the old upright piano, his footsteps made hollow sounds. Sitting down on the long wooden bench, he took off his glasses and, after hesitating a moment, pulled a small mirror out of his pocket and gazed into it anxiously. Large faun-like black eyes lent a pale fragility to this face. He checked to see that his brown hair was neat, his shirt and tie spotless. Then he replaced the mirror, put on his glasses, and waited.

It was Sunday, and three minutes to three. Outside, one of the boarders was riding his bicycle, circling the cement courtyard of the empty school and sounding his metal bell at every corner. He jumped up at the sound of footsteps. A canvas-covered cello case came in, hanging from a very white, very thin bare arm; feet in clean, worn brown shoes; bony legs, snake-like in wrinkled stockings; a long, thin body; and then a face, empty of expression.

He stood very stiff beside the piano bench, smiling with desperate fixity, watching her come to the platform and lean the case against one of the straw chairs. 'I'm sorry there are no lights,' he laughed. She looked at him once, then up at the dusty dark bulbs, and began to unpack her instrument without any further reaction.

She was the ugliest human being he had ever seen. Her body was a cage of thin white bones, slightly hunchbacked, from which short legs and long arms dangled, and a small, thin neck curved up. But it was her head which made people stare with incredulous fascination: she had thin black hair growing low on her forehead and pulled back into a severe bun, revealing that the back of her head was flat. In contrast, the whiteness of her skin seemed dead and clammy. Her eyes were small, black and round, half-shut under eyebrows that formed one straight, thick black line from temple to temple; a fainter line emphasized the upper lip of a thin, wide mouth; her nose was long and uneven, her ears large. She was not more than twenty-five years of age, but the expression on her face communicated a grim agelessness.

He looked at her with a sense of outrage – it was the same helpless anger that made him walk quickly past the dirty, bright-eyed beggar children on the street.

'There's no music stand, I mean,' he laughed nervously, cursing himself as his ears reddened.

'I see.' Her voice was harsh. She was wearing a lacy white blouse and a black skirt, and the blouse had come loose at the back. He turned away and began to go through the music books he had brought. They fell to the floor with a rustling clatter, one by one. He scrambled to collect them darting an embarrassed glance at her. She was tapping the bow of her cello against her shoe with unhurried precision.

'I have the Beethoven variations on "The Magic Plot", she said coolly, when he had finished. He nodded with exaggerated enthusiasm, rubbing his cold hands together and wishing he could vanish from the room. 'May I have an A, please?'

'A what? Oh! Oh, yes!' He laughed again, dashed to the piano and hit a wrong note.

'Oh, sorry! I ... I ...' The sound of her instrument, nasal and pompous, suited her so well that he had to fight a hysterical temptation to giggle.

'Here is the piano part.' Her gesture was brief and slow. She was exasperated and despised him beyond endurance, yet he had been brought up to be polite. He set the music up hurriedly, turned to the first page and waited.

'Page fifteen,' she said dryly.

'Oh – is it?' He gave another inane laugh and found the page. 'Thank you.' He waited.

'I am ready.'

'But we need a music stand.' 'I play by memory.'

'Will you begin, please?'

He did not know the piece at all, and the humiliation seemed to disturb his vision. When she came in, after the first two bars, he switched to a major key and waltz time, but she went on playing, and after the first few jangled moments, he began to listen. There was a professional quality about her playing, a controlled and sustained concentration, an authority of phrasing which surprised him so much that he pushed his glasses halfway down his nose. She was playing calmly, her eyes half-shut, swaying gently to the beat. He turned back, scanned the notes, and joined her.

In the sustained silence afterwards, he turned towards her with enthusiasm.

'Beautiful! I'm sorry I ...'

'May we repeat?' He thought he saw a slight smile touch her face as she said this. It intimidated him immediately and he pushed his glasses up roughly, turned back obediently and began to play. He was concentrating so hard that only towards the end did he realise he was playing alone although the cello should have come in. He stopped at once, his hands flying to his shirt collar.

'Continue please.'

After a brief moment of hesitation, he continued.

'You play well.' She delivered this token with characteristic dryness. His hands trembled on the keyboard, as he thought 'now she's going to expect me to play like – like Gieseking'.

'Shall we continue?'

By the time they had played each variation twice he was flushed and tense with excitement. A faint tinge of pink appeared on her cheeks, although her grim self-possession remained the same.

'It was beautiful,' he stammered, wanting very much to let her know how pleased he was, how very beautiful it had been for him.

'Not bad.' She addressed the back of the hall laconically.

After a pause, during which he stared at her, he sprang down and tried the light switch. An involuntary triumphant laugh cascaded from him as the naked bulbs blazed. Her reaction was to frown once against the light, before shading her eyes. He was instantly chilled.

'Does – does it bother you?'

'Somewhat.'

He switched them all off immediately. It was dark.

'Just extinguish this one and leave the others on.'

He did so with sulky obedience. When he looked at her there was a smile on her lips. He thought she looked unbearably ugly. Hostility gripped him. What was all this about anyway? He hadn't asked to play with her. She had barged in on him yesterday while he was playing a Mozart sonata and said she had some pieces she would like to play with him. In that stilted manner of hers she had made him offer to come on a precious Sunday afternoon out of sheer politeness.

'I have a slight headache,' she announced.

He muttered that he was sorry.

'I teach kindergarten here,' she continued, in the same austere tone of voice. He murmured that he knew.

Ignoring him she went on, 'My brother works at a bank. I live with him and his wife; they have two children – twins – two years old. My sister-in-law is expecting another child.'

He looked up in sudden contrition. She looked lonely, with her cello between her knees.

'Maybe you know my father,' he suggested timidly. 'He teaches mathematics here.' She nodded, looking past him.

'My brother also works at a bank.'

She nodded again. 'The same bank.'

'Really? How funny!' he laughed nervously. 'I ... I also have a sister ... younger.'

'So you are a middle child,' she remarked dryly, leaving him with nothing more to say.

After a heavy pause, he cleared his throat. 'I ... er ... I apologise for my, my behaviour about the lights.' And he turned away anticipating another long silence.

'What are your plans after graduation?' Her calm question and hoarse voice set his nerves on edge.

'I'm ... undecided,' he spoke defensively. 'I must ... excuse me ... I have to go now.'

'I do not enjoy teaching,' she continued, addressing the back wall, 'and I do not enjoy older people. But children are different.'

He expressed polite interest, took out his handkerchief to polish his glasses, and, since she was not looking, surreptitiously wiped the sweat off his face.

'There is something about children which is open and clean.' She looked at him, and he produced a guilty artificial smile; she looked away again, slowly. 'It is good when you know if ...' Her voice grew harsh. 'If you are busy, don't let me detain you.'

'No, not at all. I'm quite ...'

'Oh, it's four o'clock. Will you excuse me? You play well.'

She packed her instrument, and marched out.

He did not see the cello-playing kindergarten teacher very often, but when he did, he smiled with tense eagerness in response to her cool nod. One morning, he came across her in the cement courtyard. She was surrounded by fifteen very young children who were playing 'Oranges and Lemons', forming tunnels and trains, clapping and singing. She skipped and clapped and sang with them, her ugly face shining and her black shirt flapping in the wind. He passed them, walking slowly, fascinated by her face. A feeling of pity for himself, for her and for the whole world hurried his steps and made him stumble.

He returned to class but was suddenly revolted by the dull monotonous routine, the bored teachers and the meaninglessness of it all. That afternoon he read her unsigned note.

'My pupils are rehearsing some songs for the May Day festival. Could you please accompany them on the piano?'

The next day he met them during break. The children were noisy and excited. He sat at the piano and surveyed them self-consciously and apprehensively. She briefly indicated the order of the songs. Then she clapped her hands and there was instant silence.

'Now we're going to sing, "The Mulberry Bush": one, two, three, four ...'

The children were shrill and loud in their enthusiasm. He played the song with solemn correctness, stealing surreptitious glances at her. They went through the songs one by one with short interruptions that consisted of one tantrum and three fits of giggling, all of which were coolly ignored. Her attitude towards the children was wonderful. He felt humbled – children had always intimidated him.

The class was dismissed half an hour later. He gazed intently at the piano while she rearranged the benches, jumping up just as she finished to apologise for not having helped her.

'We shall be having three more rehearsals,' she announced. 'Is this time of day convenient for you?'

'Yes. Any time is fine.'

'Thank you.' She put out her hand. He took it and held it for a moment. When he released it, he was trembling. 'This is very amiable of you,' she added, still studying him. He realised that she had never looked directly at him before. 'If you like, we can meet here again on Sunday at three o'clock.'

He nodded, stammering incoherently. She gave him a single nod and walked away.

On Sunday she unexpectedly walked in while he was playing the Waldstein and insisted he continue, which he did, with a proliferation of mistakes hurriedly trying to get the ordeal over with. His eyes were glittering when he finished.

'You sacrifice expression for speed.' She spoke harshly, unpacking her cello. He saw that her elbows were sharp and bony, and the hair on her white arms was dark. 'You play as though someone were chasing you.'

He laughed nervously.

'Otherwise you play well.'

He wanted to reply in the mocking tone his brother would have used. Instead, he studied his hands and frowned. He was tremendously vulnerable. It hurt.

'I have brought some Bach.' Without looking at him, she placed the music on the bench beside him.

Sunlight streamed into the dark hall. He looked up from a sunlit square on the stone floor and found her small round eyes scrutinising him. As though his glance were a signal, she began to tune her cello. The loud, nasal sound awoke in him a sudden desire to jump on her instrument and break the bow over her head. He felt a bitter desire to crush her bony body with his hands. The violence of his emotions terrified him and he leaned away from her, stiff and silent.

She glanced at him briefly and then drew her bow across the strings in a long melody, her left hand a thin claw vibrating slowly, grotesquely. Finally, she looked at him, but he did not speak.

'Your sister is a beautiful woman,' she said finally. 'Perhaps she takes after your dead mother.'

He sprang to his feet, but she continued.

'You have sad eyes; you do well to wear spectacles.'

He stared at her, trying to understand the emotion within him. A ray of sunlight fell across her shoes and then dissolved.

'I think it is well to veil beauty.' A strand of hair fell over one of her large white ears.

He sat down again with his hands clasped tightly together. He was beginning to understand.

'There is beauty in little children, you see.'

Her harsh voice sounded as though she were conversing with a hidden person. If he bent forward, he could touch her hair.

'I was wondering,' he said dreamily, almost inaudibly, 'if you would like to see a film with me tonight?' He threw his head back and waited.

She laughed.

She laughed in a loud, rough cascade that became softer and softer. It sounded as though she did not laugh often. The laughter loosened her bun, for all at once a sheet of straight black hair fell to her shoulders, hiding her face.

'Would you?' he repeated carefully.

She straightened, and her gaze focused on the back wall.

'No, thank you.'

'Very well.' He did not move. The room seemed to be swaying from side to side. 'Very well,' he repeated in a whisper. He shut the piano lid and walked past her as she sat with her cello between her knees, her hair silken and black like the sudden flowering of a poisonous plant, her expressionless face white – a monstrous figure, majestic in its ugliness.

EMILY NASRALLAH

The Green Bird

For a week now, that man has been sitting on the cement block facing my building. I don't know what winds blew him our way – a strange man. But who would dare ask these days? Who would query someone at the corner of a street in Beirut? Or in a bomb shelter? Or a hideout? Who would dare question anyone, whether man, woman or child? In Beirut these days no one would ask questions like 'Who are you? Where have you come from? Why are you here?' It would be like striking a match to the fuse of a bomb.

He has been sitting in that same place for a week now, immobile, not eating or drinking, nor even moving to answer the call of nature ... Or at least that is how it seems to me. I see him every time I walk in or out of my house – there he is.

How can I avoid looking at him? He is sitting there, facing the entrance. Not crouching in a corner, not blending into a wall, not squatting behind the trunk of what used to be a tree. Just sitting. Simply sitting on that concrete block – half a metal barrel, actually, filled with cement, used as a shield by a fighter at some point during the war. (Don't ask who poured the cement into the barrel, or when or for what purpose, for that is another long story – a nine-year-old story and growing older, its action taking place in this neighbourhood and that and the other ...) In any case, that is what he is sitting on, a makeshift stool he has turned into his makeshift headquarters, from which he darts his nervous glances. This man seems to be living on the cement barrel. And I cannot avoid looking at him as I come and go. He's sitting in that strategic spot and watching me. Every time I open my door I see him watching me: every time I step out of the building, he's watching, or so I think, for I have not had the courage to make a move towards him, maybe get closer to him, introduce myself to him get to know him ... I wouldn't dare.

'Get to know him? Whatever for?' I ask myself as I slam the car door and take off as far away as possible from his piercing gaze.

Actually, that, I think, is what bothers me most about the man – his eyes. They are constantly searching, constantly roaming in all directions, in the direction of every noise or movement. His eyes seem to be bolting out of their sockets. And like a pair of nervous birds, they fly this way and that, dart up electric poles and down again, throw themselves against concrete walls in a bid to go through them. Then, realising the impossibility of the task, they return to their place, only to try once more.

Yes it's his eyes that bother me. They are searching for the unknown, the unattainable. Always looking, seeking, searching. I question his motives, and my doubts grow. Why has he chosen to take refuge in this place? Surely if he's lost something, is looking for someone, it would do him good to conduct his search walking around the city streets rather than ... Why here? Why does he not move from that spot?

Why? A huge 'why?' An enormous question mark. It escapes

me and hangs in the air and becomes part of the echoes around me. It obsesses me.

I could save myself this worry and gnawing curiosity and ask an alert neighbour – the one who lives at the intersection of other people's lives, recording every movement of their traffic. Or I could ask the building janitor.

Yes! Great idea! And so simple – why hadn't I thought of it before?

Naturally, he answers my 'why' with a smile that says he 'has it all under control'.

'Who? That man? He's one of the refugees, the displaced.'

He waits for me to ask him the very obvious next question, 'Where from? What part of the country has he run away from?'

He opens his book of war days, in which he's written newspaper headlines and news reports and radio broadcasts and analyses and rumours and stories that float in the air. 'What does it matter?' he says finally. 'He's a refugee and a stranger to this neighbourhood.'

'Have you spoken to him?'

'Yeah, the first day. He's from one of the really hard-hit areas. His people have taken refuge in the building facing ours – you know that, of course. There are twenty families. They've taken over all the empty apartments whose owners are in Europe.' Sarcasm tinges his words.

He stops there to see whether I am satisfied with the information he has provided. Then he looks at me, a pregnant, knowing look and the same confident, all-knowing smile of a simple man that says, 'It's under control, I've got it all under control.'

'Blessed are the simple people,' I think to myself. 'Blessed are their simple, uncomplicated hearts ... It is not easy in these times to be so simple-minded. Oh, how very difficult it is!'

'So, madam ...' he continues when he realises that I am not

going to ask any more questions. He continues because the story has been knocking on the walls of his conscience. It pushes him to tell it. 'The man has a story, madam. No, a tragedy is what it is.'

I object to hearing this. Immediately I stop him. 'He must have relatives or a family.'

'Yeah, sure he does. They took the second floor in the building. But he refused to go up there, to stay there. The family is made up of ...'

I interrupt him again: 'It may be the shock of having to move. He'll soon get used to it and start leading a normal life ...' I move, I shuffle. I want to run away. I have no desire to hear what happened to the family, how many they are, how they live. I certainly don't want to hear the details of the tragedy that has befallen them. It has befallen the entire country. It has engulfed us all ... What good will the details do me? No, I certainly do not want to hear this story. 'Do you hear me, man? What good are details once the whole is lost?'

'Ah, but some details are important. Some details carry within them the essence of the whole.' My simple building janitor waxes philosophical, the words gushing out of him. He no longer awaits my questions or comments.

The door is half open and I try to leave, but he stands in front of it and points to the man sitting on his barrel, his voice an odd mixture of pity and mockery. 'This man has lost his mind,' he says. 'And who would blame him, really. Man is not made of stone, you know. Some tragedies are just too big. More powerful than he is. They destroy him.'

Again I try to get away from the circle his words have drawn around me. But the door is half closed in front of me and the janitor has saddled his story and is preparing to take off on it.

'He keeps saying, "He'll be back." Do you know the story of the Green Bird? It's an old story. One of our forgotten legends told in the villages. "I am the Green Bird. I walk with a swagger." This is how it begins. You know it, the mother revives her son from the dead, rejuvenates his dried bones...'

He quotes again, 'My dear Mother/picks up my bones/places them in the marble urn ...' Do you remember? The other woman, the stepmother, had conspired against the beautiful young boy and killed him, and made his body a feast for her friends. But his dead mother's soul revived him. It gathered his bones into a marble urn and nurtured them with drops of water until they came alive again! But her young son could not return as human flesh. He turned into a green bird and started haunting the other woman in dreams and wakefulness, hovering over her, plucking at her, reminding her of her crime and that Judgment Day was near.

This man here, he awaits the return of the green bird. He says he's afraid to close his eyes lest the green bird returns and he does not see it. He stays up all night, his eyes roaming all over the place. He's afraid to close his eyes and not see the green bird when he comes.'

'Who is this green bird he talks about, anyway?' I hear myself asking the janitor, almost against my will. The story has conspired against me, and it hooks me, and I cannot free myself. 'What is the green bird to this man?' I ask again.

My storyteller smiles, an almost mocking, nearly sad, slightly humorous kind of smile, and I think, 'What is there to smile about? Didn't he say the story was tragic? Yes, but isn't there a saying that goes, the most tragic events are those that induce laughter?'

'It's his son, madam. His eldest son, his only son among five girls. He brought him up, educated him and put him through university and pinned all his hopes upon him. He sold everything he owned to put him through medical school. Yeah, he's a poor man, but he managed to put his bright son through university to become a doctor. Being bright, at least, is not the privilege of the upper classes alone, you know. God gave him a bright young boy, and through His divine guidance, the man educated the boy. He would have graduated from medical school at the end of the year. Then he would have been able to carry some of his father's burden. Maybe even put his sisters through school ... Who knows, one of them may even have been able to go to university herself. Who knows what the future would have held for the young man before the ...'

'Before what?'

I scream the question at him but he continues, calm, unperturbed. 'Yes, madam ... Before that shell found him and ... he exploded.'

The janitor shifts from philosophy to literature and waxes poetic. He draws the clearest of pictures for me and slaps me with it, using that one expression 'he exploded', with all its literal connotations. I have certainly never heard it before – war slang, no doubt. And as he continues speaking, frame by frame the scene he describes plays out behind my eyes, and I am transported to a different time and place. The scene unfolds before me, running alternately in fast and slow motion, very slow motion.

'The shell surprised him as he was coming out of the bomb shelter. He had wanted to take advantage of the calm. He thought it was a truce or a ceasefire. He told his mother: 'I'll just go out for a minute and move the car to where it'll be safer.' That's when it surprised him. First one shell then the other ... They slammed him against the wall ... That's how they found him. His mother, his father, his sisters ... that's how they found him. Splattered across a wall in a hail of shrapnel and rockets and shells. It was raining bullets as the father gathered his sons' remains into his bosom.

One entire night the man sat in that pool of blood, his son's remains in his arms. One whole night. Then in the morning they had to pry what was left of the body from his arms in order to prepare it for burial. They had to pry it by force from his arms!

He spent the entire night talking to his son, soothing him. "You are cold. The night is cold and dark. Listen to the thunder and the rain. My child is so cold. Leave him, leave him in my arms. I am keeping him warm." The neighbours had to all work together to pry it away from him. Like prying open a clam shell to remove the precious pearl in order to bury it in the earth.

Here he is now. He's lost his home and shelter and left the last of his rational mind in that pool of blood. If you go near him he'll ask you, like he asks everyone else, "Have you seen him?" And you would say, "Who?" And he'll tell you, "The green bird, of course, who else? He's coming, don't you know. Come sit next to me. He'll be here any minute now."

He says that, and he doesn't care who you are or what your reaction will be to what he's saying. He may think you're his wife or one of his daughters. He may think you're there to wait, like he is. And he will just repeat those words to anyone who crosses his path. He'll ask them if they've seen it ... ask them to sit quietly by him and wait... ask them to listen as he does, keeping his eyes open all the while ... darting from one corner to the next ... waiting ... for the beloved green bird.'

Translated by Thuraya Khalil-Khoury

Chat

We struggled to teach our children Arabic. It seemed important to retain what they had known of the language before we left the country. As parents, this issue is tragic, yet to our children it is comic since they feel such deep concern about our mother tongue is unwarranted. To them, our insistence on speaking Arabic is mere nostalgia arising from our attachment to a bygone past. They link it to the folklore and habits of the motherland and compare it to the tradition of eating hot *kishk* on cold, winter evenings.

'Cool! It's cool, our Arabic, but what's the big deal?' they ask. This attitude, which we hear so often, confirms our suspicion that language to them is no more than a series of fragments – halves and quarters taken from many different languages, including Arabic.

'But, dear, what about our language?' I ask my son. 'Don't forget it's what you heard as a child back in Lebanon.'

'Sure thing! Our mother tongue is cool, really cool,' he mocks me in Arabic. 'We're using it right now, aren't we?'

This is as far as you will ever get in such a discussion. It is unlikely that your son or daughter will be interested in further debating a seemingly incomprehensible subject that clearly means so much to you as a parent but little to them. Actually, Arabic means a lot to me. When we left Lebanon, my son was ten years old. To me, Arabic is the harmony I created while communicating with people in Lebanon. Yet my son's language has obviously been imparted to him by the world he inhabits.

I used to think that we appropriate the objects we own vocally, that the paraphernalia we use in our daily lives responds to the very sounds emitted by our vocal chords. My son, on the other hand, believes that the objects we have to leave behind only belong to the voices that happen to call to them, to vocalise their names. That's why I write and he paints.

Sometimes I wake up in the middle of the night and find my son sitting in front of his computer screen. 'What are you doing?' I ask, intrigued. He tells me he is chatting online with young men from all over the world. They use virtual names and addresses that only turn real after an online friendship develops and confidential e-mails are sent.

I sit next to him, my eyes glued to the screen. He tells me about Internet language and explains that he chats with these people using a coded language of acronyms and abbreviations that Internet users are apparently familiar with. Ban, he tells me, actually stands for burns, and ASL stands for the age, sex, and location of the interlocutor he is talking to. This is basically a new version of English, interspersed with other languages and simplified in its phraseology so as to facilitate communication between people living in different parts of the globe.

'Is this the new global language?' I ask in dismay. 'Of course not,' he quickly replies, assuring me that this is only 'chat' language. In the blinking dialogue box on the screen, a steady stream of racist profanities is being exchanged by my son and his Swedish chat buddy. I start arguing against the vicissitudes of Nazism and white power groups but my son gives me strange looks that make my concerns seem naïve and out of place. This rabid Swedish Nazi could very well be our sweet Arab neighbour who owns a grocery shop in the adjacent street. Foul talk could simply be a way to escape boredom under the protection of online anonymity. 'Mom, this is just chat. You don't need to start fussing again.'

Once, I caught him chatting up his best friend in Lebanon, using a fake name and the same foul language that his Internet pals are so fond of. He laughed and said that chatting has become an addiction among the young in Lebanon today. I wonder how much Lebanon has changed over the years. People who have never left the country are now able to travel vicariously through the Internet to a world of 'chat', where barriers crumble and rules cease to exist.

Translated by Sleiman El-Hajj

Nazik Saba Yared

Improvisations on a Missing String

Saada, wrapped in a robe, sat in her hospital room waiting for Suha and Anwar. It was eleven o'clock and they still hadn't come. She glanced over at the window. Maybe the heavy rain was holding them up. Her eyes fell on the bed that had been stripped of its sheets. Two weeks had seemed like two months and now she must stay at home for two more. And what about her students? The doctor had ignored her question. His only concern was her recovery.

'Sorry we're late, Saada. Anwar is still trying to park the car.'

Suha's voice brought her back to reality.

'I don't want to add to your problems while you're in the hospital, Saada, but there is something you have to know,' Suha said abruptly.

'What? Has the doctor discovered something he's kept from me? Will I never go back to my students? Will I end up in agony like Mama?'

'Don't worry, it's nothing like that. It's just that we're going away.'

'Again?'

'For the last time, God willing.'

Saada didn't understand.

'For the last time? Why?'

'I'm never coming back to this country. Even Anwar is finally convinced. We're going to Canada.'

Saada was at a loss for words. Was she going to lose her sister again? And this time forever. Would she never see her after today? What had happened? She tried to control her agitation.

'Do doctors earn more in Canada?'

Suha's smile was bitter. 'He can't practise medicine there, his medical degree is not even recognised in Canada. In any case, it's no longer possible for him to practise here either.'

The sisters fell silent. Then Saada asked: 'What will he do there?'

'He's going to look for an administrative job in a company that sells medical supplies.'

Saada was dumbfounded. Anwar's patients were so important to him. She couldn't believe it!

'What about your art, Suha? People here know you and appreciate your paintings.'

'I started here as an unknown artist, and I succeeded. I can make a fresh start there as well.'

Saada wanted to say how extremely competitive it is in the West; that it is almost impossible for Arabs to break into the art world. 'Does an artist remain an artist if torn from her roots?' she asked instead.

Suhai's answer was abrupt. 'My roots? I don't have any roots here. Maybe you have roots, maybe, but I don't. Even Anwar's a stranger here now. The war stripped us of our rights. There are no laws to protect him and no government to uphold any laws. Look around you! Who's looking out for us? Armed thugs, that's who!'

'So this is the reason you're leaving?' Saada asked sadly. 'Then it's true that politics corrupts everything it touches.'

'If you mean my life,' remarked Suha aggressively, 'it was corrupted a long time ago and politics played no part.'

'But politics made things worse,' Saada said to her sister. 'Don't make Anwar the scapegoat.'

'The Lebanese war made him a scapegoat. And he made me a scapegoat long before that. Besides he's only concerned about his work and his patients.'

She choked on the last word and Saada noticed tears in her sister's eyes.

'He loves you, Suha.'

Suha let out a strained, sarcastic laugh. Did her sister not notice that their relationship had changed, how Anwar is no longer the person he used to be?

'Yes, he loves you! He works day and night to provide you and Nadia with every comfort.'

'He lives day and night to attend to his work. He has no emotion or concern left for me.'

Saada looked shocked. But Suha ignored her sister.

'Is love having a colour television, a bigger fridge, a new car? Is love valued at tens of thousands of liras, and not one penny of affection or concern?'

Suha choked on her humiliation. Love to Saada was always weighed in terms of a person's qualifications, position and income. What did Saada know about love? She read about it in literature, in books. Love! She only loved herself!

'Always so idealistic! You live in the world of literature so how can you know anything about life?' Suha said disapprovingly.

'Have you forgotten how much in common you and Anwar have and how much love and understanding there is between you?' Saada saw the look of hatred in Suha's eyes.

'If it was love, it has certainly faded.' Suha was now unable to hold back her tears.

Anwar removed his outer layer of clothing, put on the white surgical gown and entered the operating theatre. Throwing a quick glance at the anaesthetised patient on the operating table, he washed his hands and put on the surgical gloves that Samiya was holding for him. Then he bent down so that she could tie the surgical mask around his nose and mouth. Samiya began sterilising the skin around the patient's stomach and waist while Anwar selected a suitable scalpel. He leaned over the body stretched out in front of him, his fingers probing to determine where to make the incision. Suddenly he heard commotion outside: his hand froze as the door behind him flew open and something hard was thrust between his shoulder blades. 'Stop what you're doing and take the bullet out of our comrade,' ordered a harsh voice.

Before Anwar realised what was happening, two armed men had pushed the operating table away, and dragged in a table on which lay a young man covered in blood.

'Get a move on! Our comrade has a bullet in his chest. Take it out!'

The hard object was suddenly pressed into his back even harder. Then he heard his colleague Saad shout: 'Are you crazy? Get out of here right now!'

'We're not leaving and if the doctor doesn't perform the operation immediately we'll kill him,' replied an insolent voice.

Was this a nightmare or reality? Anwar found himself surrounded on all sides by fighters, their guns aimed directly at him. He didn't dare look at their faces. Through the heavy atmosphere of terror came Samiya's soft voice: 'Get out. We'll operate on him but we have to remove his clothing and sterilise the wound.'

'We will leave as soon as the doctor starts operating.'

Anwar used the scalpel to cut away the shirt from the clumps of mud and coagulated blood. When the shirt was finally removed, blood began to gush out.

'Stethoscope!'

Samiya quickly handed it to him and the armed men began to leave. The wounded man's heart was still beating, but the beats were faint and irregular. 'What if he dies under the scalpel, and what if I don't operate on him?' thought Anwar. But the hard object between his shoulder blades ended his speculation. Samiya began to disinfect the man's chest while Anwar reached for some sterilised forceps. He smiled as his eyes fell on the anaesthetised patient who would regain consciousness before he had finished operating on the wounded man. He didn't know whether to laugh or cry when he inserted the scalpel and forceps into the young man's chest.

Removing the surgical gown that seemed to cling to his perspiring body, he hesitated for a moment before opening the door. The thugs would be waiting for him.

'Well, Doctor?'

Six armed men were blocking the corridor, and behind them stood two women, one old, the other young. His heart started to pound rapidly.

'Did you remove the bullet?'

'Yes, thank God.'

And thank God their question hadn't required him to lie. Now there was only one thing to do. They moved aside to let him pass: then they burst into the operating theatre. He dashed over to the stairs and ran down. Soon they would know that the bullet had damaged the heart, torn through an artery. There was nothing he or anyone else could do. He entered his office, grabbed his briefcase and rushed home, determined, as he returned the concierge's greeting, that this would be the last time.

Translated by Stuart A. Hancox

Najwa Barakat

The Language of the Secret

It was still dark outside when Khaldoun woke up. His mother was fast asleep. Her snores, heavy and intermittent, sounded to her son like waves breaking softly on the shore or the singing of a boiling kettle. He opened the door slowly, careful not to make any noise. The door resembled a lion opening its wide jaws and yawning loudly. His mother tossed in her creaking bed, trying to find a comfortable position. The boy grudgingly made a mental note to oil the hinges the following morning. Closing the door behind him as swiftly as he could, he exhaled deeply and leaped out into a night that was only too eager to embrace him.

He stole a quick glance at the sky before fixing his gaze on the ground. This was the night before the full moon appears, the night when the sky loses its shine as the light from the stars begins to wane. When he reached the well, he turned right and counted the fifty steps that would lead him to a large rock under which a few days ago he had hidden a bag with secret contents. Khaldoun's heart was beating frantically against his chest and he felt a bout of vertigo closing in on him. Now wait a second! He still had plenty of time to kill, didn't he? Yet his feet forced him to rush ahead.

The rock was certainly less heavy than it was, but that was probably because all his senses had been so mobilised for his mission that a heavy rock now seemed to him like a small pebble. Opening the bag quickly, he carefully emptied its contents onto the ground. In what appeared to be a ritual of some sort, the boy undressed and placed his shoes and clothes neatly in the bag before returning it to its hiding place under the rock.

'Lord, this is how you created me,' Khaldoun said standing completely naked in the darkness. He felt a strong urge to remain like that with the soft breeze caressing his skin, rubbing against him endearingly like a family cat. If someone were to spot him then and there, the onlooker would have fled the site immediately, mistaking the well-built boy for a genie out of a fairy tale. The bucolic people in the countryside were, after all, quite gullible folk. Such a strange sight would have seemed to them a hallucination, created in a moment of divine wrath. A cold waft of air stung Khaldoun's cheeks, so he set to work immediately. The ritual was completed by wrapping a long cord he had removed from the bag around his waist, leaving his hands free to engage in the task ahead.

Soon he felt suffocated and out of breath. The cord around his waist cut into his flesh, making breathing difficult. Khaldoun removed it but then put it back on again making sure it would not hinder his breathing this time. After all, this was not part of his plan.

Thoughts of his demanding and overbearing mother gnawed at him, eating at his insides like worms that feed on human flesh. Some days she would bless him and kiss his face, saying she was privileged to have such a wonderful boy, such a strong man. Yet if a day passed when the food cupboard was empty because Khaldoun had been unable to find a job, he would automatically become a stigma of ingratitude and shame to his widowed mother, who depended on him. She would say that even his dead father must be angered by his son's irresponsible behaviour. His mother's tirades seethed continuously in his mind as his naked body moved silently into the night.

Suddenly, a chill ran down his spine. He stopped in his tracks and covered himself with the crude rag cloak. At first, Aadla had been reluctant to make the cloak for him, but eventually, when he threatened to leave, she yielded to his request and asked him the inevitable question: why did he want a woman's cloak? Then she volunteered to make him a proper jacket embroidered with silk thread, but the boy had refused and with a piece of charcoal he sketched the crude cloak required.

'You must be out of your mind, Khaldoun!' The girl was exasperated with what he had drawn on her bedroom floor. 'This thing looks like the uniform of those fraternity people,' she protested. 'It doesn't even have a hood or buttons.'

But Khaldoun persisted and Aadla finally agreed to make the cloak of rags and not say a word about it to any living soul.

Unhindered by the tiny pebbles that bit into his feet as if to stall him or lead him in the wrong direction, the boy proceeded under cover of darkness. He carried his secret and was eager to meet whatever destiny awaited him at the end of his journey.

Translated by Sleiman El-Hajj

The Hot Seat

When he hurried to sit in the seat the plump woman had vacated, he was only thinking of his tired legs and feeling glad that no one had pushed in front of him as usual. The seat had become empty without warning since, unlike most women, she hadn't started getting ready for her stop much too early.

The seat felt hot, but it had nothing to do with the blazing heat of the sun which was beating down fiercely on the roof and windows of the bus and flooding its interior.

He had a vision of his mother and sisters trying to air public seats before they sat on them, either by fanning them with their hands to chase away the odours of the previous occupant or by turning over the cushions. Whenever he criticised them for their misgivings, one of them would remark with disgust, 'Who knows what minute traces are left on the seat from the person before?'

It was a strange warmth, accompanied by a dampness he could feel through his trousers. Seemingly the woman's thighs had rubbed against the plastic and left it sticky. All at once he remembered the like dark pools of sweat under her armpits; and he thought of their source and of the flesh there, which was without a doubt soft and delicate.

The man shifted around a little and spread himself out on the seat so as to make the heat penetrate and reach along his extremities. Then he brought the palm of his hand up to his nose: it must have picked up the smell of the woman's perfume when he had inadvertently grabbed hold of the seatback in front of him. He found himself unable to move, even though the bus had reached his stop. He remained lost in thought, wishing that he could have the chance to meet a woman like her, in that prim and proper country.

As the bus sped on, his imagination kept pace. He was only occasionally disturbed by the voices of the other passengers mingling with the songs of the radio. Then a more aggressive voice cut into his thoughts, the sound of someone spoiling for a fight.

'Aren't you ashamed, you pimp? Pervert! Degenerate! Heathen!'

The voice came closer. Surely he wasn't the reason for this savage outburst? Not even the most skilful clairvoyant could guess what he was thinking. But he turned around, curious to see the owner of the voice, which was now close up to his ear. He was met by a violent punch, rocking his head, making his ears sing and his nose pour with blood, and leaving him gasping for breath. The harsh voice shouted again, ordering the bus driver to stop. He didn't know how he came to be pushed so hard that his face hit the side of the bus, how he was sent rolling down the steps and lay sprawled in the dirt, where the men crowded around him, hitting and kicking him, egged on by the same harsh voice.

'Don't you have any sisters? Where's your shame? How can you disgrace a respectable woman in broad daylight?'

Translated by Catherine Cobham

Etel Adnan

The Power of Death

It was raining hard when he came to see me and we both looked through the windows and commented on Parisian summers, hot and so often wet, and we agreed that they have a way of breaking one's heart as if for no apparent reason. We tried to talk about something cheerful but somehow everything seemed bleak and we gave up. We looked at each other, and we could have been lovers, for we had been friends such a long time that the air between us was always standing still.

I will call him Wassef, because that's the name he should have had – don't ask me why.

While the rain stopped and the sky remained dark I made him a cup of coffee. I tried to put on the radio for some music but he showed such displeasure that I stopped searching for a good station. He told me, in the form of a question, that he was on his way to Stockholm. 'Do you know that I'm going there?' he asked, and went on talking.

Suddenly I was sure that he was going with the single purpose of looking for Erica, and I didn't speak much. It rained again, and then the sky lifted, just a bit, just a shade, and we couldn't find things to say, and eventually he left, leaving the door slightly open. I had no reason to cry; but I did.

I later learned from him that he searched frantically for Erica but couldn't trace her, and that just when he was resigned to go back to Damascus he received a note at his hotel from a relative of hers whom he had contacted, telling him on a little piece of ordinary paper scribbled in black pencil that Erica had died, exactly two weeks before his return to Stockholm.

Wassef's tone of voice over the telephone belonged to a man who was close to losing his mind. 'Come back to Paris,' I suggested, 'and let's talk it over.' He went on rambling and for one long hour he reviewed the main events of his youth. Yes, he studied in Sweden and met Erica when they were at university; yes, they discovered love together, and she was a virgin when at the end of his first year at the School of Engineering they went north and didn't sleep for days and made love as if the hours didn't exist, with the curtains drawn, their bodies quivering with fatigue and happiness.

One would think that there is nothing new to love stories, but Wassef was recalling his life with such intensity that the world was being created anew through his pain, although sinking also in an abyss of frightful proportions.

I knew that when he got his degree he had left Erica, returned home and eventually got married. But his wife had died in childbirth and he remained in his parents' house where they helped him bring up his child. He used to come to Paris quite often, but had never returned to Sweden.

His voice over the phone was hard to bear, his sorrow was too cruel; in fact, cruelty was hurrying in through the windows until I felt I would suffocate. I begged Wassef to come immediately so I could be reassured while taking care of him. 'Don't worry,' he said, 'I'll write you a letter.' He hung up.

As I knew him too well, I filled in the spaces of his life. He convinced himself, for years, that he had forgotten Erica, as he never liked to burden himself with feelings of guilt. He also had some excuses: for years his country had experienced incredible upheavals; revolution and repression had been his daily bread for so long that he never allowed himself the luxury of a past. And now, like a door slamming in his face, the past was catching up with him.

His letter arrived:

I am walking through transparencies night and day, and each time I stop I discover a particular moment of the life I had with Erica. Sometimes she walks near me, like she used to do, and the sun creates shadows under her eyelashes and she looks at me, a bit later, stares at me while we sit face to face to have lunch, and in the afternoon she lies on our bed and she takes her time and then we lose ourselves in each other and I carry her voice within me and I hear it now telling me she loves me and I believe her, now more than I ever did, but then I know she died recently, as her cousin wrote to me, and I refuse to go to her grave because I'm afraid to imagine the state of her body in it, and it is hot and luminous outside while I write you this letter, but I have to tell you that she just came in and she's playing with my hair and the smell of her body is filling the place and it's overwhelming me and I may faint any moment as I may also never send you this note.

But listen. Never in my life have I felt that I could lose control of my reason but I do now because her life and her death are mingling and I don't know where she really is, if she's hiding somewhere on this earth or if she's really dead; then where is she and would I ever find her if I died too, but this universe is so big, so vast, so out of reach in its infinite dimensions, where would I have to go to follow her and find her and see her once more, beg her forgiveness, and please my heart, see her once more, a minute, a second, a fraction of a second, once, just once, even if she has to appear as a ghost and frighten me and fill me with bliss, come under unbearable lights or in the deepest darkness that my eyes and my mind could sustain.

His letter went on and on, becoming utterly desperate, bringing no order to his emotions or to his thoughts. Often he was delirious, mixing the present with the past, speaking of hallucinations, threatening suicide. He also described the weather, carefully, obsessively, the Swedish summer he remembered and the one he was again experiencing. Here in Paris the rains were hot, as if the skies too could be irrational, and I read and reread his pathetic words.

He called again on the phone, asking me to go to Stockholm and see him, saying: 'I need somebody here who can understand the pain I'm going through. I need you.'

I turned in round and round in my flat, went to the Luxembourg Gardens, drank coffee after coffee ... I had no choice, I had to go to Stockholm. I left a message at his hotel, booked a room at the same address and made a plane reservation, giving myself one more day in Paris before my flight.

I am one of those people who still links Sweden with Nordic legends and black-and-white movies, although the night before I left I went to the Champollion and saw *Niagara*, that old Marilyn Monroe flick which throws together a lot of water, passion and doom. I saw the many close-ups of Marilyn's face and wondered if each of her films was not about her own destiny. She played her own role: I watched, until fiction became real, and she left behind her the image, repeated ad infinitum, of our own impossible loves.

It wasn't planned as such, but it was the real beginning of my trip.

I won't say that I was happy to find myself in Stockholm so suddenly. Wassef is dear to me, yes, I was worried and eager to see him, but travel in the European summer has about it something deflating: Europe is European in the winter, it always seemed so. Since early childhood in Damascus I viewed Europe as a land of grey skies and frozen fountains, with a lot of electricity shining in the night. But what of Stockholm in the summer? A city which sizzles in a country considered cold, a no man's land subverted by melancholy, the monstrosity of sunshine on the heart's deserts.

My hotel room was comfortable, but Wassef was not there. He had left a note telling me that he would be back soon. He didn't say what he meant by 'soon' – a few hours or much longer.

I waited. I turned on the television, but other than the Grand Prix Formula One races there wasn't much that I could understand. Of course there was the news, and I could watch what I already knew. The Grand Prix was fun: it took my mind away from Wassef for a few laps. Schumacher won the race and there was his trophy, followed by Germany's national anthem. The guy who came in second was utterly miserable. The whole thing was taking place in Belgium where it was raining: the cars were sliding and the energy flowing. It all looked like science fiction but it was real, for all that reality's worth.

I had lunch, then dinner, at the hotel's coffee shop. I tried to read Michael Sell's work on Ibn'Arabi – I'd been in the middle of the chapter on the 'Garden among the flames' before I left Paris – but it was useless: my peace of mind had been shattered. I drew the curtain tightly and tried to sleep, but light continued to seep through. I remembered past tiresomenesses, but that was of no help. I knew that I was in the middle of an endless luminosity and that the day was stretching on until midnight, ending where the next one was waiting ... I didn't sleep the next day either, and the third went by, anxiety filling my time like rising water. I couldn't even get myself to be mad at Wassef and return home.

One late afternoon, a knock on my door: Wassef was back. He stood before me haggard, crazed, shaking, the whole of his being solidly engulfed in some irradiating darkness that was made particularly conspicuous by the extra glare of light that his entrance brought into the room.

Oh, why did he arrive in such bad shape! He didn't excuse himself for his absence, didn't ask if I was worried or angry with him. He remained contained within his own world without making the slightest effort to reach out. He smelled of alcohol and sweat and the bad odour of defeat. After a moment I said: 'Wassef, please sit down on this chair,' but he paced the room, alternately opening the curtains, looking out, and closing them, until I asked him again, this time more firmly, to take a seat. At last he sat down on my bed, took off his shoes, then his jacket. He was wearing a pink shirt which I shall never forget, partly because it endeared him to me, and partly for some other reason I couldn't define.

'Please, keep the light out of this room,' he begged, and remained silent afterwards. I drew the curtains together as closely as I could and lit the lamp, but the electricity was useless for we were sitting in an endless twilight.

'Where were you?'

'Nowhere.'

'I am here for you, to help you, if you need me.'

'I never needed anyone.'

'Well, I'm here, we can talk.'

'I have nothing to say.'

'No, it's not true. I will need a lifetime to repeat it again, to say it all, and I can't, of course ... Do you believe that I ever had a life?'

'Wassef, try to answer your own question.'

'Yes, I had a life, I have one, and it's miserable; I'm probably going mad and I don't know it.'

'You are not in any danger, I would think. Just tell me where you were these last days and then we'll start.'

'Start what?'

'This story about your life.'

'My life ended long ago,' Wassef said, 'long ago, the day I decided to go back to Damascus, but I didn't know it, it took me a lifetime to realise that I was dead, a ghost seemingly happy. Erica cried and she was sweating, her hair all wet, her face like under pouring rain, and she was looking at me intensely, and kissing my face, falling into a deep silence, and then weeping, again and again, like a newborn animal, and then everything stopped while I felt paralysed, wondering if I would ever get out of that room, that tiny space in which I experienced incredible happiness, a sort of bliss which used to turn into a warm current feeding my veins, and her skin was soft under mine, and her breathing even, soft like her voice, and I was lost in her hair, and in between her lips, and my heart was beating, it was a messenger bringing good news, and her legs were long and smooth and always warm and, even in the dead of winter, she was burning and radiating a slow, steady fire, and here I was, pulling myself away from it all and her own blood was receding towards her chest and she looked pale and her breathing was becoming difficult and I started looking at the door and she understood that it was over, for no reason, it was all over for her, and for me too, and I don't know how I went through that door never looking back, never to see her again.'

It was obvious that something had broken down within Wassef, a sustaining wall, a dam, something was pouring forth that nothing could stop, so I had to sit and wait and listen to this old friend, this man who was racing back to his youth, erasing some forty years of his life in order to reach the two or three years of intense happiness he'd experienced. Erica's death broke his will to pieces, and the deeper truth that he had hidden so successfully from himself was shining now to shattering effect. He'd never stopped loving her, but it took her ultimate disappearance for him to come back to her.

I decided to go out for a while, just walk. I asked him to stay and wait for my return or go to his own room, but he remained numb. I opened the door, went down a couple of flights and met the street with relief. I came to a corner café and gulped down two tall mugs of beer, soon realising that it was the last thing I should have done, as the beer reinforced the effect of the grey luminosity that was sticking to the walls. But I drank some more, thinking it would help me to sleep.

When I got back, I found my friend spread out on my bed. He was barefooted, with his shirt unbuttoned, staring at the ceiling. He didn't move when he heard me come in. Suddenly, like a snake, he threw a question, startling me: 'We only see things that don't exist, don't we?'

Then he went on: 'Now I know for sure that I won't lose her again. In her solitude, she is mine, all mine, forever, like before, years ago, as if it were yesterday, and that she's here, in this room, facing me, then moving around, yes Erica, we shall go to Uppsala, do you remember the summer we went, sometime in June, you are in Queen Christina's Palace, that grey hall we visited, and you're sitting on the throne and I am the Ambassador from Syria, I brought you perfume and dates, you will wear the one and eat the others, and everybody knows I love you, they're looking at us, and then we went to our hotel room, we made love, and I tried to do it again, you told me you were exhausted by the trip, the heat, the light, but I tried again, I thought that would help you fall asleep and you were fighting the light and got nervous, and so did I, and we started to turn on our bed and you made little sounds and I was fighting some invisible element, it was the light intensified behind the shutters, pressing itself, and you were burning with fever, begging me to stop because you loved me, and loving me was enough, and we didn't need to make love on and on when she could barely breathe, and that my own energy had been spent, and our eyes would stay open, and then I put my head in the hollow of her neck and tried to rest and she laid her hand on my back and we were outside the limits of time in a country with a never-ending summer which wears out its lovers as if they were meant to be doomed.

And listen, listen to me, I left her. I ran away. By the end of that summer, when nights started to return to relieve us of the sun's power, when things had a chance to brighten up, I told her, with no warning, like a thief, a coward, a traitor, that I was leaving the very next morning for home. That night, while making love, she cried, and didn't say a word but kept quivering, she didn't kiss me but remained placid like the sea's surface on an August morning, she stopped crying and looked at me for a long time, for ages, and she got up before me, earlier than usual, not having slept, she dressed, made coffee, I ate and she didn't, didn't even take a sip from her cup, and a few hours later I found myself on a boat, and she was standing on the quay, and then I never saw her again.'

'And now,' I interrupted, 'you're back, after all these years, or where are you? Why did you suddenly think of her, what triggered all this pain, these memories?'

'These are not memories!' he shouted. 'You must realise that the past has come back, that something has disappeared, I mean the years between the moment I left her and the moment I was told that she had died. She is here in front of me, young and full of the future, she loves me and she's my universe, the whole of it ... and I will never sit facing her, laughing, drinking in her presence, abolishing anything which is not her.

I am today the man I should have been, now that the walls of the kingdom have fallen down and that she's invisible to all but myself, after having received all these messages that she kept sending these last years, telling me that she would die and give this earth back to its wretchedness.

But what did I do? I lied to myself. I looked for women, intensely, taking advantage of the travels that my work required, in many European capitals I paid women to spend nights with me and thought that I was satisfied, until that night in Berlin, about a year ago, when I picked up a young girl about the same age as Erica when I left her. The girl was new to the streets, shy, embarrassed and embarrassing. I don't know why I kept asking her to repeat during the night that she loved me. 'Please keep telling me you love me,' I begged, and she kept saying it in German, then I taught her to say it in Arabic, she said it, then reverted to German ... and fell asleep. In the morning she told me that I was a strange fellow and that it should have been obvious that she couldn't love me, like that, just like that, and when I told her that I knew it well but that I needed to hear that sentence so that something in me could believe it, or half-believe it, she kissed me gently on the forehead, refused to take my money and left. An hour or so later I gave that money to the woman who came to clean the room and she thanked me many times, and I tried strolling aimlessly in the streets but nothing worked, then I dealt with my business and returned to Damascus certain that I was a man destroyed.'

I tried to distract his mind and suggested that we take a walk, but he complained about the persistent summer light. Then I said let's go and see a film, and that suggestion turned out to be disastrous, touching some raw nerve. He plunged deeper into a world all his own, his voice trembled and he continued:

There was in the Damascus of my childhood a cinema – do you remember? – where you had to go down a few stairs, and in there – I was twelve – I entered a universe of beautiful women, they were not women but magic, unattainable, private, all for myself. I saw Jean Harlow then Marlene Dietrich – the most impressive ones – they were blonde, as silky as a river's surface, and I would come home with fever then take one with me in my bed, the first women I had aged fifteen or sixteen, I made love to the most enchanting images in the world, and I would cling to my sheets which were as smooth as the screens on which they appeared, and disappeared, and they haunted me in the classroom, their pictures hiding in my books. The world was full of them, I thought, I will grow old and travel and join them, which one I didn't know, but it will have to be in a place like in the films, with stairways, moonlights, music playing in the background and stopping when we are kissing. Then I left with a scholarship for Stockholm.

When I met Erica she belonged to the movies, she created an atmosphere overheated with tension, the promise of unending nights and surrender, and this became true, my dreams granted as to no one else, her body had a horse's madness, she would smile and her smile would change the weather, draw me in, her teeth were the frontier of my happiness. And one day I gave her up, for what, I don't know. I would give anything to know what really happened, in which one of my soul's layers ... I buried myself in Damascus, in work, then in a marriage which was interrupted, as you know. I entered the pitiful routines of visits to whorehouses, in Madrid, Hamburg, Amsterdam, cheap versions of my childhood cinemas. I was spending an hour or two with women whose names I wouldn't even ask, doing intimate things and never seeing them again, I was leaving with a heart blank and stilled, worrying about such things as train schedules and business appointments while I was even forgetting that I was still alive.

Wassef couldn't cope with himself. Sweating heavily, getting red in the face, he was becoming incoherent. His monologues were signals of such desperation that they made me slide and sink into a strange sadness made of sympathy and fear, and my inability to absorb his pain made me feel hard and inadequate. At some point I managed to persuade him to return to his room, and I remember the panic in his eyes; but he turned his back, opened the door and moved his heavy frame out and down the stairs. The next day I called him and there was no answer: the reception desk informed me that he had gone out quite early but that his belongings were still in his room. I was happy that he hadn't checked out – he was just away. That same day I decided to return to Paris, and wrote him a few awkward lines to let him know that I had to leave and that he could always contact me at home as usual. I felt a bit shameful. I was running away. I tried to convince myself that by having stayed a couple of weeks in Stockholm for his sake I had done all I could and hoped that he would follow me to Paris or go back to Damascus now that there was nothing he could do, nor anyone he could see with whom he could talk about Erica.

Once in France, not a day went by without my trying to reach him. He was not there. One day, at last, I was told that he came to his hotel that very morning, took his baggage and left – they had no further information. I felt utterly cut off. The summer, I thought, had indeed ended.

Then one dismal and rainy morning I found a letter from Wassef in my postbox. It was posted from Stockholm and written in a troubled hand. I went up to my apartment, waited for a while, tried to do a few things, made some calls, washed some dishes, put on some music;, but nothing would alleviate my confused fear of this unopened envelope ... Then, I read:

Dear, dearest, I'm here, and you're my only friend, you know it, you've known me for so long, you remember the days when Damascus still had a river, and we loved it, it was a galloping torrent in the winter, and now they've covered it with the same kind of cement that covers their souls, but my own soul, where is it, where, do I have one, who am I? I have to talk to you about Erica, you'll understand, since her death everything is so clear, crystal clear, her death has brought an excruciating clarity upon the world and now that I know that she isn't here, it's late, always too late, it's useless, I know that only love matters, absolutely so, and how can I tell her that she freed me, by her dying, that now

I can love her, as she did then, back then, she loved me as I love her now, and I'm hurling my head against a wall, her absence is a wall and I'm breaking myself against it, dearest, I'm suffering beyond anything I ever knew, beyond what one can bear, the world is flat and silent, there's so much light, this dead light of Sweden, which is unbearable, I am alone with her and she's a ghost, lying there in her tomb, starting to rot, and they wouldn't tell me where she's buried, I won't touch that grave anyway, I will have to have it opened, it will make her death real, it would, it's as well that I don't know where she is, she's everywhere, here, in my head, my eyes, in front of me, once in a while she comes in my sleep and never stays for long, and I am given back to her absence.

I have to let you know something I did, like an ultimate effort towards total illusion, and at this point I can't understand if I'm a monstrous being, if I had always been a wicked failure hidden behind what people called my gentleness, but we have to come to the point where we know who we are and why we did whatever we did, and if it could have been otherwise, where did everything go wrong, or is it rather that things had to be what they have been, and in both cases it's terrible, it's maddening. I could have had a long life with Erica, come every night to her bed, her body, her presence, her luminosity, and I lost her by my own doing ... Good God, was it impossible from the beginning, given who I was, a young man with no sense of the future, no means to think other than of the passing moment, tied by ancestral timidity, and defeat must have been inbuilt in me if I had to turn my back on the only happiness I experienced.

I want you also to know something of the nightmare I'm

going through. You see, when this love for Erica surfaced, engulfed me, it possessed me with such a force that one afternoon, when I saw myself in the mirror, I looked young again, with the face I had when she and I were together, clouds and turmoil crossed my eyes, women were staring at me in the street and I felt that I could conquer any of them, as I did for a period of my life, and I found out that it is precisely because you are madly in love with a woman who is absent that you can most likely say yes to any other adventurous one, thus desire becomes a fire that will burn any piece of wood, and that did happen. I met a young woman while I was at the coffee house. She was sitting at the table next to mine. She smiled and I answered her call, I was feeling young again and we walked aimlessly until dinner time, but the summer light lingered on, and getting tired, I invited her to come to my room and she accepted, and then it happened, I enveloped her with my desires, my passion for Erica appeared to be meant for her, and I let the poor girl believe so because I needed to believe it too, and we made love furiously.

I moved next to her own place, she was going to the university and I was waiting all day, dreaming simultaneously of two women, mixing their images, and sometimes crying.

For the first time in my life I felt grateful, unreservedly, allowing myself to be disarmed, but I didn't let my heart feel sorry for this young person to whom I knew I would never give much of anything and I wasn't embarrassed to be living as an impostor. Things just happened, instant after instant, and I was watching her when I noticed some stormy ocean within her blue eyes and a broad smile breaking for no reason whatsoever, and she was moving her head on the pillow, pushing back her hair without touching it; then I became a traveller on an unknown road, at a crossroads I took a side road and I was with Erica again, looking for her under the skin of my new conquest. It was both awful and exhilarating, I thought that a dream of resurrection could only be fulfilled by death, the death that had already happened, it was all over, and possibly something else would break through, a disclosure, the resurrection of time, the repetition, the sacred repetition of what had been sacred, and new ideas rushed forth, they interfered, they required an answer. In the heat of my spirit's wilderness, while I was kissing an innocent face, suspicions arose, I wondered if Erica had done anything to have inhibited me and that I had stored in my mind's deepest recesses. Would it be possible that she had been the source of a desperation that I felt and never formulated, did she make me sense from the beginning that our relation was transient in essence, an absolute with no roots in this world? Must I bear my guilt alone? But I know, I know that she loved me desperately, totally, like a cloud loves another cloud and merges into it, why must I keep playing a game, now, when I'm under her death's absolute power, having lost the very notion of my own self? ...

Yes, we went dancing one late evening, the air was motionless, the sky a canopy of fog and indifference. We found a little place where youngsters were drinking and there was a jukebox and I found an old tango and we danced while I was aware that the young people were sneering at us, at my greyish hair; and then a small miracle happened, I found an old American song which used to be Erica's favourite, a smashing success back in the fifties, it was 'Kiss of Fire'. She often danced alone to this tune, with such independence in her body that I went crazy with envy and desire while she moved, sure of herself, enjoying her power over me, but my partner was hearing this music for the first time and she liked it because it seemed to please me. We danced some more, and came home, and I watched her eyelashes which at a certain angle made shadows on her cheeks, and her eyes looked as if through a veil, and I wondered if she wouldn't give me at last the illusion that Erica was alive, in my hands, just for a while, just for me, even if it had to be only for a fraction of a second.

The next day I bought a dress, a deep blue silk dress with little flowers on it, and in the evening I gave it to her and asked her to wear it; she giggled and looked beautiful, and we went out and drank a lot when something suddenly upset me, heavy showers descended over my soul and we hurried home. Once in bed I fell asleep immediately and dreamed of doors which remained closed while dead fish were being unearthed from a patch in the garden that my grandparents owned in Damascus. The following day my body kept shaking not with fear but with apprehension, I tried to eat lunch but had just coffee with a cheese sandwich, and felt old. Then I was seized with the frantic desire to find the perfume that Erica used to like. I needed it. I searched in many stores; a French perfume quite famous in the old days, our days. I found out that it was still on the market, the salesgirl threw a strange glance in my direction, and I bought the little flask and waited impatiently. That evening I gave it to my little girlfriend, my mistress, she asked, 'What's this again?' I replied that I had just bought it casually, and I lied by telling her that I was indeed eager to discover its smell.

I opened the bottle. I could as well have opened a tomb.

I sniffed. The perfume was heavy but mixed with a lighter one. Its scent seemed, at first, neutral, then it spread and made me feel disoriented, dizzy. It was slightly nauseating. When she rubbed some drops on her skin I entered Erica's smell like one enters a chapel or a vortex – and this young woman smiling at me was not aware that I was using her to recapture a ghost. I pushed her onto the bed, my urge becoming violent, confused. I was at once unspeakably happy and desperate. I had entered again the chaos of love, its matrix, holding my breath and breathing it, holding under me a woman who was real and alive while making love to a phantom, until that absence mingled with the present to recreate the primordial night ... My eyes closed, their lids fused, so that I could see that resurrection was happening, that I was recovering my sense of ecstasy ... Erica's body was pulsating like neon lights all over mine, as well as over my young lover's, and I was growing old with this perfumed and innocent body, while in my mind emanations of death were gradually and irrevocably being mixed. I was begging salvation from this abused woman. I poured more perfume on her, renewing an old addiction, trying to recapture that state of bliss that I used to know with Erica, wishing that Erica was there, and mine, for one night, at least, one long night lost in the ocean of time, and I called 'Erica!', and the young girl shook me off her body and cried out loud with bottomless anger that I was now taking even her name from her, and giving her one which wasn't hers, but all I knew with unbearable clarity was that Erica was lost forever, that time had indeed lapsed, that I was only an old man with a knowledge now so useless that it had to be thrown into a wastebasket, and I came close to killing her. I think I did it, within the smell of death, sniffing like an animal and pressing hard at the top of her breast, at her neck's tender line, I was pressing so hard that her face was obliterated from my sight, I was sweating and licking her perfume which was turning sour, I couldn't tell if my young victim wasn't sleeping forever, like Erica was already doing. I was learning with that same unbearable clarity that to kill is just another way of crying, blood replacing the flow of the tears.

My dearest, I could go on and on with this letter, even if it were only to postpone the moment when this is over, this conversation with you, this agony. Listen, I told you that I won't visit her grave, but there's no grave for her, that's what I learned recently, it's hallucinating, they took her away from me, for sure, they cremated her so that I can never find her, never, and so many forces are fighting around my head, all of them invisible, so I don't see why I should go on living ... and still, I am in a state of prostration and while you read this letter I may very well be under arrest, or thrown into a world lonelier than a prison cell, hopelessly devoid of any horizon. Yes, all threads are broken, the tiniest ones too; we'll have total darkness again. I'll remain in this city for a while at least, getting out of my hole just to prowl the night. There must be a wisp of smoke, some particle of hers that I can breathe, they burned her and her fumes will be eaten by me, swallowed, made one with my flesh, I will descend, Oh God help me if you exist!, I am not Orpheus but I will follow her, somewhere, and she won't be there, I know, I'm sure, but I'll keep searching. She used to call me her baby, but that baby died long ago, and that's also going to be true of the old man I am now, the sooner the better, here, or in the underworld, I'll drown in my sorrow, I don't know, I don't want anything, I can hardly move, but

I will stay although I'm already left with nothing, I mean nothing.

I went through this letter. I read and re-read it, then I opened the window, later read it again ... and Paris was soft and in the dark a thin rain was wetting the air and I phoned Wassef's old hotel. I needed some connection with Sweden, with him, but have been told that they haven't heard from him for quite a while, and, just to add something, I asked about the weather and they told me it is still fine. Anyway, I know that the summer is over and that the Swedes are about to start their long descent into winter and its uninterrupted darkness.

ALAWIYA SOBH

Stories by Mariam

I remember exactly when Ibtisam decided to get married.

She had tears in her eyes that day we met at the café near the crossroads of the Central Bank and the an-Nahar Building on Hamra Street, a landmark where businessmen and intellectuals gather at pavement tables that surrounded the fountain. This is where Ibtisam and I met in the autumn of 1986. On that October morning we chose a table on the outdoor terrace that was still damp from the morning's cleaning.

Ibtisam's mind was not clear and her face reminded me of murky water. She had tears in her eyes and her words were heavy with desperation as she spoke about her loneliness and hopeless desire to be 'in' instead of 'out'. She told me that the night before our meeting she had watched a romantic Arabic film, the kind she used to make fun of when she was a rebel who believed that such stories were unrealistic and useless, when she looked at the world through a black-and-white lens.

She told me how she choked when the hero put his arms around the woman he loved and gazed at her eyes. She was moved by the tender romance that she once thought passé. She asked me many questions: 'Did these revolutionary men think we were ready-made whores imported in rebel cans? When someone is defeated, are they also defeated in their politics, love and dreams? Why were we, women, so trusting in our attempts to find new dimensions and spaces in which to put our dreams, bodies, and feelings that become so cruelly exploited? Were we twice as disappointed as the men we thought liberated because they sought freedom for us and for themselves, when all along they suffered from split personalities and harboured archaic caricature images of women in their minds? Were we women realistic in our dreams or did we also have split personalities, concealing in our rebellious bodies a concubine? I don't understand: was it all a lie then? I really don't understand or know,' she kept saying. 'I never lied, and I am sure that many of those who died or were defeated also did not lie. But then, why were we defeated? Is it because we were really liars or because we were brutally honest?'

I don't know. All I know,' she said, 'is that today I am lonely; lonely like never before. I also know that I need the same kind of love I saw in last night's movie, even if it was just make-believe.'

Ibtisam told me how deeply saddened she had felt a few days earlier when she tried on her new lacy nightgown before going to bed. She had looked at herself in the mirror from all sides, contemplating her bare breasts. But when she slid under the covers she felt a strange tightness in her breasts although they were free from the constraints of a bra. She cupped them in her hands and stared at them for a long time before turning off the light and falling asleep.

Barely two months after our meeting, Ibtisam decided to get married. It was around five o'clock on a cold afternoon, the sound of raindrops 'as big as stones' – as my stepmother, joining three fingers together, described them – were thudding on the ground. When the phone rang I was in my room, tracing the contours of a new dress from *Burda* magazine in order to save some money, pass the time and treat myself to a new outfit for my next meeting with Abbas.

I was surprised to hear Ibtisam's warm voice on the other end of the line asking me hesitantly if we could meet for drinks that evening. I was elated at the prospect of seeing her after such a long absence, especially when she said she had missed me. It's been a long time since anyone said they missed me, including Abbas, who only said it to me once at the end of every month.

It was pitch dark outside when I opened the door and stepped out of my house and into the stairwell on my way to meet Ibtisam at Modka Café on Hamra Street. I wondered, as thunder roared in the distance, what Ibtisam needed so urgently to tell me.

We sat at a table next to the large window overlooking the street below. It was just after five, if I remember correctly, and the rain was heavy. I sat there trying to warm my hands on my hot teacup while Ibtisam swirled her glass of vodka with a glimmer of expectation in her eyes.

She told me that she and Jalal had decided to get married. He had proposed to her countless times and she listed all the reasons why she should marry him. While she said this, Ibtisam watched the passing cars with her hands tucked into the sleeves of her white pullover. She said he was a good man and that their marriage was based on a rational decision to build a life together and be equal in all matters.

'Isn't family more important than love, now that love is gone and we were defeated in all we attempted to achieve?

Should I stay forever 'out', out of each and every circle, even out of my own life? And what will happen to me if I don't get married? Will I ever be able to love again and get involved in a new relationship?'

'No, absolutely not,' she said answering her own questions. 'I shall now love the man I intend to marry. I am so tired: I need a man who accepts me, truly loves me, and who will care for me. Jalal has been waiting for a long time and I need to be loved by a man who will take me to the point of no return: I need to go there so that I can shed my fears, and maybe this can only be reached in marriage.'

'But you and Jalal are so different!' I insisted.

'I am surprised you think that. Jalal is well educated, loves life and has experience in politics.'

'He does?' I asked.

'Well, he tried working with various political parties at one time, although now he has left politics and is completely focused on his job. Besides, Jalal is open-minded and liberal; isn't it enough that he thinks my life before him does not matter? From now on we will make decisions together.'

'How about Karim, does he still mean anything to you?'

'I'd rather not speak about that, it still hurts. Besides it's over: Karim is out of my life now and I don't want to look back.'

The hope in her eyes and the reflection of the white pullover on her face dissipated the fear lurking in my heart. I was able to breathe easier as I felt Ibtisam was in control and no longer infatuated by dreams of dust. Deep down, however, I was worried that she thought of Jalal as a knight in shining armour who could rescue her from fake love and illusive happiness. I feared that, once again, she might only find unhappiness at the end of this road.

Ibtisam's love of life was different from mine. She wanted to inhale it, taste it, and live it to the fullest, singing her heart out, like a brown bird, so that life can sing back to her. For Ibtisam, in spite of her outward strength and occasional stubbornness, was a romantic, a warm and child-like individual who sings and flutters like a bird in the hands of men like Karim, who know how to love her unreservedly.

I remember how her love affair with Karim started at university during the early war years. It was as if another 'Ibtisam' was born right there and then in front of my eyes. Her eyes, voice and body became pure femininity. I remember her vividly in her tight blue jeans, her white open-collared shirt and the black cardigan she used to tie around her shoulders.

She would wait for Karim and me at the cafeteria in the Education Department. Leaning against the old juke box hidden in a dark corner, she tried to decide which of Fayrouz's old songs best suited her feelings that day. 'Oh Handsome One, How I Fear Losing you', was her favourite. She played it over and over again, while her eyes spoke those same words to Karim. Sometimes she would pick 'See How Vast the Sea Is: This Is How Much I Love You', and her eyes would also sing along with Fayrouz.

I saw how the bright light of love danced in her eyes and how her cheeks flushed with warmth whenever she spent time with Karim. She played with the buttons on his shirt and looked at him with intense playful eyes that said, 'I love you, I love you.' Karim would smile broadly, lean towards me and mutter, 'Look how crazy your friend is!'

Karim did not belong to any political party, although he came from a Christian family that had ties either to the Communist Party or to the Syrian Nationalist Party. He was, however, always wavering between these two parties, although his secular outlook made him closer to the leftist parties that had coalesced together to form the National Movement.

Before the end of 1970 Karim went to work in Saudi Arabia, after falling victim to a sectarian kidnapping in the Ras al Nab'a area of West Beirut. He was stopped by a couple of men manning a security barrier who asked to see his ID card. When he showed it to them, they forced him out of his car and took him to an unknown destination: a card he carried indicating that he was a member of the Patriotic Movement was useless. During the three days he was detained, Ibtisam almost lost her mind with worry: she neither slept nor ate, but drank endless cups of black coffee and chain-smoked. Her worry was compounded by an incident she had witnessed the day before Karim was abducted. At the Barbir Bridge she watched armed men pull two individuals out of their car before savagely throwing them over the bridge to the street below. They died instantly.

That night she stayed awake sobbing and throwing up as if to eject the horrible scene from her memory. The image of the two men's bodies haunted her, the perpetrators' evil eyes seemed etched on the walls of her bedroom. She kept hearing their voices: 'Yalla, these guys are for throwing away. Today we will eliminate the same number they killed yesterday on the other side.'

She remained paralysed by fear until Karim was released and put on a plane to Saudi Arabia, where one of his relatives had found him a job.

He took to long absences, returning to Beirut once a year on short visits. All year, Ibtisam would wait impatiently for his return. When he appeared, her whole body breathed the odour of love. She wore make-up and dresses instead of jeans and her restless eyes became soft and calm.

In his presence she spoke in whispers; but once he left her voice became loud and high-pitched as she shouted 'I love you, I love you,' over the bad telephone lines.

In 1982, as the Israeli army surrounded Beirut preparing to invade, the city sustained constant and heavy bombardment.

That night, with water so scarce, Ibtisam managed to find one bottle to wash with. As she walked out of the bathroom wrapped in a towel, the phone rang. She had no idea that Karim had been in Beirut for two weeks but as soon as she heard his voice, she shouted: 'Karim, is that you? When did you come and how? How long have you been here? Is it really you? I can't believe it: where are you?'

'Here in Beirut.'

'When did you arrive? The airport is closed.'

'A few days ago, but your phone line was out.'

'Liar, when we don't want to talk to someone we use the phone line as a pretext. If you really wanted to contact me you would have found a way or come over to see me.'

'Anyway, I want to see you.'

'When?'

'Now.'

'Now? Are you crazy?'

'Yes now, I want you. I want a woman, not any woman, I want you.'

Her silence lasted only a brief moment.

'Ok, but how? Bombs are falling everywhere. Besides, what can I tell my parents?'

'Think of something.'

'Pick me up in half an hour.'

It was already past eleven when Ibtisam slipped into the seat next to Karim. The city was unravelling like a string of beads under the Israeli shelling. Karim drove off hurriedly, oblivious to the falling bombs. As for Ibtisam, Beirut seemed to gleam like a ring of precious stones.

Once their hands locked together she was no longer angry. In fact, she forgot everything. She held his hand and kissed each of his fingers, moving up to his wrist, then his neck and his face until they came to the house of a friend who had escaped to Paris.

Karim lit candles and distributed them around the house: he then pushed the table to one side so they could sit on the floor. He held Ibtisam's face in his hands and kissed her with pent-up hunger as she wrapped her arms around his neck and hid her face in his chest. They moved in unison when he lay over her, his upper body fusing into hers while his lower body lay between her open legs which gradually and firmly closed in on him. He unbuttoned her shirt and released her breasts, covering her nipples with his mouth. With sweat dripping from his brow he asked, 'Can you take off your clothes?'

Ibtisam removed her shirt and lay down again. Karim undid the buttons of her jeans and pulled them down.

A few seconds later, he let out a strange laugh. 'Hey, how come you're still a virgin?'

He did not know the answer to that question because they had never spoken of it before. Then he laughed again in a manner that disturbed Ibtisam. 'Is this at all possible for a rebel like you?'

'Karim, why are you talking this way? Why should rebels not be virgins? Besides, you know that this is my first relationship. Your senseless questions are bothering me. Just like you wanted me, I wanted you. Are you upset that I slept with you?'

'No, on the contrary. I'm very happy you did, but maybe we should have done this a long time ago.'

'But why are you interrogating me?'

'I'm not. Are you crazy? You are my love – I'm not interrogating you, I am just happy to be with you.'

When he took her back home at daybreak, a mantle of darkness still covered the city and the black birds of death circled overhead, their screams intercepting the sound of bullets. Ibtisam rolled the car window down, stuck her head out and shouted at the miserable and vast city night: 'I love you, I love you.'

Then Karim spoke to her about the 'vein', a vein he had felt throbbing in the back of his head and neck as soon as he was released from captivity. This vein was telling him: 'Get married Karim.'

That day he told her that he loved her, although the vein told him he should marry someone from his own religion and kinfolk. It was the vein talking, not his heart, a vein so powerful that he did not have the energy to resist it. This is what he believed and this is how he explained it to Ibtisam, who could only stare back at him, her eyes round with disbelief.

She hid behind her silence not knowing what to say. The overwhelming injustice tasted bitter in her mouth. Karim continued speaking, but she no longer listened, her ears only registering the sound of her steps as she walked away from him.

Ibtisam drained the last drop of vodka in her glass and said: 'When we were young we believed that life was tailored to suit our needs. Unfortunately, we soon discover that we are the ones who must change.'

She then repeated her decision to marry Jalal, and this is exactly what she did.

Translated by Ellen Khouri

IMAN HMEIDAN YOUNES

The Story of Warda

When I was about to leave our apartment in the Gulf, Sarah put her thin arms around my neck. She did not want to be separated from me. My husband Rachad, on the other hand, wanted to get me to the airport as quickly as possible. On the plane, I thought I saw Sarah's hair. She has golden, curly locks like her father. I jumped up from my seat and ran down the aisle toward the first-class compartment, knowing she would be there waiting for me; but she was not. How could she possibly have been? I looked around me carefully, scrutinising the face of every passenger. Sarah simply wasn't there. She had disappeared like a magician's handkerchief.

When the fighting intensified, my friend Maha came to stay at my place. Every time the ceasefire ends and fighting resumes, I wait for her. In fact, I dream of her company so as to break the monotony of my loneliness. Sometimes I even get the urge to take her in my arms, to hug her tightly. At night we sleep pressed against each other. We are not intimidated by the shelling. Every time she comes over, I open my photo album and show her my daughter's pictures. It has been two years since I was forced to leave the Gulf and return to war-torn Lebanon, two years since I've seen Sarah. She was eight years old at the time. Every summer I beg Rachad to let her come to Beirut, but he won't hear of it.

Recently, my other friend, Josepha, took me to the shrine of the Virgin Mary in Dekwaneh, where the Virgin began to appear in the winter of 1986. I had been planning to visit her for quite a while. You see I was sure that if I begged her enough she would hear my prayers. That night when mass ended, Josepha took my hand and briskly led me to the Naf'a roundabout.

We had to walk through a crowded and dark alleyway. A soft breeze was blowing small bits of humid soil into the air as people's feet sank deeper in the muddy ground. I took my place at the end of the line. There I stood very still. All eyes were glued to one spot, to the familiar silhouette inundated with celestial light. She did not look back at them. Instead, she searched for me among the crowd and fixed her gaze upon my face. My cheeks turned fiery crimson and I felt like a hot cloud of boiling vapour. My heart hammered fiercely against my chest while bitter tears ran down my cheeks.

I tried desperately to make my way through the crowd in the hope of touching her. I stretched my hand toward the holy figure, but was petrified by the seemingly forbidding light that seemed to emanate from her reflection on the icy glass pane behind which she stood. Have all my tears, all my suffering, all my anguish been necessary for her to hear me? For a few more seconds, I could feel her looking at me and then I stopped seeing her altogether. Why does she appear to me more clearly in my dreams? Why is it that suddenly I can no longer discern her face, the colour of her eyes? She must dislike being surrounded by so many people. Still she looked at me and I'm sure I heard her whisper, 'I am with you; fear nothing and remain here!' The thought of her words intensified my sobs. 'Holy Mary, Mother of God, deliver me from this torment. Give me back my daughter.' At first, I could only hear my own impassioned voice. Then the Virgin Mary calmly said, 'Sarah is here in Beirut.'

'So it's Najla, my sister-in-law,' I screamed to Josepha. 'Najla has kidnapped my daughter. I've known it all along. Now I'm convinced that Najla has lied to me. She and her brother must have agreed to never let me see my daughter again.'

'My daughter is here,' I say to Najla the next day.

Her reply is prompt and malicious: 'I swear you're mad, completely mad.' **GALWAY COUNTY LIBRARIES**

Why does she keep saying that? And why does the wife of the concierge hold the same opinion? I remember the day I gave her husband money to buy some grilled chicken for my dog. 'Take Blacky for a walk and feed him the chicken,' I said. Blacky never liked the concierge much, but after being cooped up in the apartment for so long he was happy to leap down the stairs after him. The stupefied man paused a moment on his way back to show the chicken to his wife. 'Give it to me! Give it to me! The children will eat it. The bones should be enough for the dog,' she yelled. 'That poor woman is completely mad.'

I am scared of growing old alone. So old and wrinkled that Sarah will not recognise me. I am Warda, Warda who has suffered greatly, Warda who brought a child into this world but is prevented from seeing her. Will we ever meet again? Will she place her face against my chest and inhale the smell of my skin as she did when she was little? I remember how she used to close her eyes when we cuddled in bed, 'I love the way you smell, Mummy.' I wonder if she misses me. What if some foreign nanny has erased her memory of me?

Suddenly the phone rings. 'Hello? Hello?' I say frantically, but there is no answer. 'Hello?' I say again to the silence on the other end. I never get an answer, yet I hear breathing. Perhaps it's Sarah's kidnapper? He must have wanted my daughter to have a word with me and then changed his mind at the last moment.

'Hello ... This is Warda speaking ... Please let me speak to Sarah? Sarah, this is your Mummy.' There is static on the line and then it goes dead.

Translated by Sleiman El-Hajj

The Fragrant Garden

The neighbourhood of Gemmayzeh, just beyond Beirut city centre, was too close to the demarcation line during the war. As a result, for twenty years the area had been left pretty much to its own devices. While the war raged on, its ancient alleyways and traditional houses were abandoned or occupied by cowering people who had nowhere else to go.

For various reasons, the reconstruction that followed the war did not quite reach this quaint quarter either. Some of the old houses were renovated and transformed into expensive villas by an enterprising woman who was keen on both charging rent and preserving what little heritage remained in Gemmayzeh. Apart from that, the area remained untouched. One evening we were invited to the home of some friends who lived in the area overlooking Gemmayzeh. When we arrived we found them sitting in the garden with their guests. It was a lovely October evening, and the air was heavy with the scent of jasmine.

As is often the case when Beirutis get together, the

conversation somehow managed to turn to the war years, even though the war ended some fifteen years ago.

'The other day my daughter asked me if the war had left any scars,' said a lawyer who had shuffled back and forth between Tripoli and Paris. 'It seems her teacher had been discussing post-traumatic stress disorders and the problems faced by the lost generation'.

'What did you tell your daughter?' asked an attractive artist in her forties.

'I was taken aback by the question, actually. I didn't think that I was scarred. But then my daughter asked me a curious question. "What about *Teta* (grandmother)? Did the war affect her?" Suddenly, I started to weep because when my mother had died during the war I was unable to attend her funeral.'

'I feel like I wasted my youth,' said the artist. 'I still can't account for those fifteen years of war, or even the years that followed. Many of my friends never married, and in our culture women marry young.' Then she turned to me. 'Where were you during the war?'

'I stayed in Beirut.'

'Here in Gemmayzeh?'

'No, I lived in West Beirut. I moved after I got married, but by then the war had ended.'

'I went to Paris soon after the war started,' said our hostess. 'I couldn't risk staying. My son had just been born and my husband was able to relocate his work. I know it must have been a horrible time to be in Lebanon.'

I thought for a moment. 'There was much that was terrible, yes, and yet, in an odd way, it was a unique experience. I have never lived as intensely as I did during the war.'

'Intensely?'

'Perceptions were heightened, experiences were more vivid. I can't explain it. I felt I was really alive. I wrote poems mostly, that were compact and intense reactions to what was happening. I looked forward to going to school, to spending time with the kids I taught. There was heightened meaning to our everyday lives. In fact, I haven't felt that way since the war ended.'

'I remember the summer of 1989,' my husband said. 'I was one of the few people remaining in Beirut. My wife's family had gone to the US and left me the key to their apartment, on the sixth floor of a building in Zarif. I had offered to feed the cat and water the plants while they were away. My sister and her family had gone to the mountains in the north, and she too had a cat; so she left me the key to her place on the seventh floor of a building about a ten-minute walk from the Zarif apartment. I lived on the eleventh floor of a building in Kraytem, about a half-hour away from both houses. By then the war had been raging for fourteen years, and, although I'm a Maronite, living in West Beirut was the only choice available to me.'

My husband was keen to share his war experience. 'The shelling that summer ravaged the city. Fuel was scarce, and basic amenities were unavailable, but I soon developed a ritual. Because the electricity was cut most of the time, I had to walk down the eleven flights of stairs before heading to the Sporting Club where I would swim for an hour. The beach was the only place I could have a shower, albeit with brackish water, since there was no running water in any of the flats. Occasionally I played chess with some of the regulars there, but mostly I donned my mask and flippers to go skin-diving, relishing the cool serenity of the Mediterranean,' he explained to the interested guests.

'Every afternoon I walked to my sister's house as there was very little fuel and taxis were a luxury. Once there, I climbed the seven flights of stairs to her apartment, fed the cat, walked down again and headed to Zarif to do the same thing. It was a thirty-minute walk back to my building and, once again, I had to climb up eleven flights of stairs to my apartment. I developed different ways of making the trek up the stairs easier. Sometimes maintaining a steady, slow pace helped preserve energy. Or counting backwards and focusing on how many floors were left rather than how many I had climbed,' my husband continued.

'In the evening, I would often meet my neighbour, a gnarled and gruff Sunni, on the landing between our two apartments; it was the safest place to be during heavy bouts of shelling. Like underground garages, these spaces became the community centres of wartime Beirut. People who barely acknowledged each other before the war began to spending long, intimate evenings together, united by their need for preservation and survival,' he said with a distant look in his eyes.

'My neighbour and I found we had a lot in common. We had long discussions over bottles of whisky in the dim light of a battery-powered lamp. Confidentially he would tell his friends that he really liked his Maronite neighbour. 'An excellent young man, were it not for his name!' The guests in the garden chuckled. My husband's name literally means 'the Maronite'.

'Funny thing about all this is that when the horror of the shelling stopped, and a ceasefire was agreed upon, eventually leading to the end of the war some months later, I was miserable,' my husband admitted. 'Many of the people who stayed behind had the same reaction. Instead of feeling relieved or overjoyed, I was upset, lost. People returned from wherever they had taken refuge. Normal life resumed, but I couldn't take it. My space was suddenly invaded by all the people returning from cities where normal life is taken for granted. They had no idea what every shell hole in the wall or every pothole in the street meant. The pace of life quickened and became banal. People were busy again. It actually made me nauseous.'

Our host shook his head: 'and here we are fifteen years later still coming to terms with this devastating war'.

The delicate jasmine blossoms shivered in the breeze, wrapping us in their fragrant perfume. The white flowers fell gently in our laps as we sat silently in the fragrant garden, an anachronism in this city of unruly concrete.

RENÉE HAYEK

The Phone Call

Something was wrong that morning: she was slower than usual and her colleagues wondered why she had greeted them differently. They looked at her for some time before returning to their usual conversations. She ignored the chatter and tried to focus on the sweater she was knitting. When the telephone rang she lifted the receiver and pushed a button on the switchboard to transfer the call. Then her hands went back to knitting. Something was definitely wrong. In fact, she regretted coming to work because her hands were shaking and she had to stop several times. In the past, time meant nothing to her. The heavy bombing had shattered the monotony of time. She and her mother would select a suitable corner and turn it into their safe house.

She stopped knitting and stared at the switchboard. Transferring calls always made her feel good about herself. She could sense what the call was about from the voice at the other end of the receiver, the eagerness or fear of a lover, the loneliness of a mother whose children are far away. When unable to transfer calls, fear gripped her and she would not dare look into the eyes of people on the street. She felt she had let them all down by adding more worries to their already overburdened lives. Some voices became familiar, and she was able to give each voice a name, to imagine what profession they were in, the problems and sorrows they faced. At home, she would tell her mother about these people, and, from time to time, her mother would inquire after a caller she had not mentioned for a while.

The voices of her colleagues sounded sharper today: they looked older and paler. It was as if she had not seen them in years. Last night she had received a call. When the phone rang she and her mother were immediately gripped with fear and panic. Nobody ever called them unless there was a death in the family. The phone rang for some time before she picked up the receiver. The voice on the other end seemed to be coming from another world.

'Yes. Seven is fine with me.'

She stood motionless with the receiver to her ear long after he had hung up. It was some time before she was able to answer her mother's question, and when she did, it was only to mention his name. Her astonished mother remained silent for the rest of the day. She did not even try to get more information from her daughter. In fact, she pretended to have forgotten about the phone call.

For the past ten years she had lived without daring to think about her life. She could no longer remember how she used to be. She and her mother had stayed in their house after everybody else had left the neighbourhood. Even when the few remaining neighbours tried to convince them to seek safety in the shelter, they had refused. They would sit silently in a corner for days, never even bothering to change their clothes. When there was a ceasefire, her mother stayed in bed complaining about her usual illnesses, high blood pressure and rheumatism. She too felt sick, and complained to her mother about the nagging pain in her hands and feet. Even her fingers ached.

Her bed was right next to her mother's. It had belonged to her father, who passed away years ago. Every night after their fat-free, salt-free and sugar-free dinner, they complained about their numerous aches and pains before falling asleep. The next morning, if the weather was sunny, they woke up feeling better. Some time ago they had decided not to drink coffee in the morning because it gave them stomach cramps. She no longer remembered whether it was she or her mother who felt the cramps first. Shortly after that they stopped putting lemon in their tea.

Most afternoons were devoted to knitting. She would knit dark-coloured sweaters, some with buttons and others without, for herself and her mother. With time, their sizes had become identical, and she no longer knew which clothes were hers and which belonged to her mother. Occasionally they remembered her deceased father and indulged in exaggerating his good qualities and influence on others. They tried to hide their jealousy, for the roles of father and husband had merged after his death, and now they both needed to claim him.

Despite her initial hesitation she made up her mind to go to work, but she could not stop thinking about her seven o'clock appointment. His voice sounded in her head, and she imagined that everyone around her could hear it too. But they were all deep in their own conversations. Soon she gave up trying to relax. Instead, she kept looking furtively at her watch. Long ago, she had known this anxiety, the anxiety of waiting for someone or something. She would try on all her clothes to make time pass quickly but usually ended up wearing the same dress she had on. She could not tolerate another minute. Restlessly, she glanced at the switchboard, grabbed her black bag and walked out. Nobody even noticed that she had left.

She did not lunch with her mother. So great was her need to be alone that she completely ignored her. Instead, she went directly to her old room and sat on the edge of her bed. She hadn't slept there since her father's death. Today it was bathed in sunlight, and the pink bed covers seemed to belong to some other girl. She imagined herself in happier times as she searched in her wardrobe for a dress that would accentuate the curves of her body. She could hear herself laughing while he whispered gentle words in her ear. Her laughter used to be spontaneous: joy made her as light as a feather. When night fell and as the battles raged on, they used to sit close together at the top of the stairs, with her head resting on his shoulder, long after her mother had gone to sleep. Not even the neighbours noticed them holding hands and hugging.

Then one morning she watched from her window as he loaded luggage into the family car. She had refused to say goodbye and, when he glanced up to see if she was watching, she had immediately disappeared. After he left she couldn't even cry, she slept for days: his departure was like a sudden death. At the time she said nothing to her mother, but it was not long before she withdrew from life. Eventually they both became obsessed with the tales she told about the people whose voices she began to recognise over the phone.

Through her window, she could see his old flat in the building across the street. She smiled as she chose a simple blue dress, the dress he liked. After closing the curtains, she struggled in vain to get it on. In the mirror her sagging breasts, swollen stomach and thick thighs were clearly visible. Slowly she slipped her black skirt and dark sweater back on.

His voice over the phone was like an earthquake shaking her world. In her dreams he remained handsome, gentle, smart and cheerful, but what would she say to him after all these years? Finally she decided not to say anything. It would be better to listen to what he has to say, and laugh out loud when he asks if she still loves him.

First she stood in front of the mirror brushing her hair. Then she sat down for a minute before going to fetch some make-up from her mother's room. She applied a thick layer of foundation over the wrinkles on her forehead, under her eyes and on the corners of her mouth. Her face looked shiny, and a thin film of oil stuck stubbornly to her skin.

She went back and sat on the edge of the bed away from the mirror, as if resting after a long journey. When she looked at her watch, her heart jumped. It was already five o'clock. She showered, selected a matching sweater and skirt, dried her hair and let it fall over her shoulders. Suddenly a great sadness overwhelmed her. Why had she failed to notice that her hair was turning white?

Would she really laugh when she saw him? She practised smiling, as if smiling was something she had forgotten how to do. But something was holding her back. Perhaps he will not notice her when she enters the room. He might keep staring at the door, expecting her to walk in any minute. Even if she looks straight into his eyes, he may not recognise her. Why should he? She has acquired a sad look that is unfamiliar to him. It would be best to stand at a distance, to catch a quick glimpse of him and then leave while his eyes are still glued to the door.

She undressed and placed her clothes on the bed that used to be hers. When she entered the adjacent bedroom, her mother didn't ask any questions. Nor did she comment on her daughter's nakedness. Getting out of bed, she placed a woollen shawl around her shoulders and tucked her into bed as if she were a small child or an old woman. A few minutes later, she could hear here crying.

Translated by Mirna Haykal

Pieces of a Past Life

The day began like any other. The warm smell of fresh bread drifted through the kitchen. Soumaya was preparing breakfast as usual. He remained motionless for a moment, his eyes gently closed, gathering his strength for yet another day as he mouthed a silent prayer. It was difficult to give thanks for a hopeless life, he thought, but it was a life nonetheless, one that he was obliged to continue, so he resigned himself to another morning.

'Hajj!' Soumaya yelled over the spluttering sound of eggs in the frying pan. 'Are you up yet?'

He was like a grandfather clock, old but still incredibly punctual. There were certain moments when she could almost glimpse the father she used to know instead of only the fading pieces of a man she had loved and idolised. The person who took his place, this broken, helpless creature in the other room, was a stranger to her and she to him. His face was unrecognisable, his beautiful features buried under that haggard exterior. In difficult times when she found she could no longer cope, she closed her eyes, forcing herself to see that familiar dimpled chin. As a child she used to trace the way his lips curved into a smile with her tiny finger. But his eyes! She no longer recognised his eyes. He didn't even see her: he simply looked past her with that vacant stare. Now his sole preoccupation was that school of his across the street where he had taught so many years ago. The bedroom window was his portal into that lost world. With glazed eyes he stared out for hours, and Soumaya knew that little could be done to reach him.

She stirred the scrambled eggs in the pan, cursing as the oil splattered onto the kitchen floor.

He lifted his head slowly off the warm pillow. Steadily, and with the same calculated precision he employed every morning, he reached for the cane propped up against the side table and walked over to the corner basin near the large window. He breathed in gusts of refreshing lavender. The school gardener had been planting lavender for years. In fact, very little had changed. The moss that blanketed the walls grew in irregular patches, the same cats crawled into the same holes along the hedges, and the graffiti, scrawled messily in white chalk, still covered the same pavement. And now the same bell rang once again, signalling recess.

It was a deep jingling sound that seemed to echo against the very walls of his room. Soon it was followed by laughter that beckoned him closer to the window. He looked out, lost in reminiscences of his past life.

'Hajj! Move away from the window!' Soumaya anticipated his every move. His routine and his obsession made living with him exceedingly predictable. 'Keep it closed unless you have your sweater on!' she yelled, with little hope of being heard.

He edged even closer. Children were dancing around

happily in the garden as the teachers looked on. There was a huge gap in the fence, so supervision was essential. A lone figure caught his eye, a child playing football on the grass. He kicked a ball up into the air, bouncing it off his knees then chasing it in circles around the garden. Yet each time he kicked the ball he strayed closer to the edge of the pavement. The supervisor had failed to notice him, neither had anyone else on the street.

Soumaya stacked the dishes on the kitchen counter. Swiftly and mechanically she arranged a platter of cheese and vegetables. Whatever could be salvaged from the eggy mess in the frying pan, she placed in the centre. A tattered photograph in a worn-out frame stood on the marble counter. It was a relic of her past life. She glanced at it, recalling the family outing she had memorised down to the last detail. It all seemed so distant to her now, distant and yet so familiar. She shoved the plate roughly across the counter, cursing loudly as it knocked the photograph to the floor.

The child continued to chase the ball, edging closer and closer to the street, oblivious to the immediate threat of cars speeding past him. The old man gripped his cane tightly and his heart beat faster as he continued staring out of the window. All of a sudden the ball flew into the street and the boy ran after it.

Soumaya was busy picking up the pieces of a past life that lay shattered on the kitchen floor. The slithers of thin glass crunched under her slippers. The photograph, crinkled but still intact, lay on the floor behind her. She could see it without turning around. Tossing the glass into a bin under the sink she turned slowly to face it. It lay there silently, and she almost expected her loved ones to come back to life.

Laughter fills the empty corridor and echoes off the walls that

*are plastered with colourful hand drawings and messy collages.
They're laughing at her as she fidgets with the camera, pressing
the buttons, tugging at the lens, trying to follow the directions.
They're calling out to her. Her fingers are unsteady with her own
laughter as she yells at them to keep still. She concentrates and
steadies her hand. She's wasting time. The students will soon
arrive. Father must get back to school.*

She bent down slowly and picked up the photograph.
Hesitating for a second, she marched over to the bin and
hurled it in with the shattered glass. It was all over now: there
was no going back.

Suddenly a deafening sound startled her. A car screeched
to a halt on the street below. Soumaya was overcome with
an immediate sense of panic. She searched the house calling
his name; but there was no reply. Rushing to the corridor,
she caught sight of the open door. In a flash she ran out of
the house and shoved her way through the crowd, her entire
body tense in anticipation. She feared the worst. *Why did I
leave him? Why did I leave him?* She could smell it again, that
burning, suffocating smoke.

*It blinds her eyes, but she forces them open. She pushes
forward, shoving, shoving through the hysterical crowd. Where
is he? Screams and sirens surround her. The smoke gets thicker. A
woman grabs her arm. Her face is vaguely familiar, but nothing is
registering in her mind, nothing is making any sense. The world
is spinning as she nears the school. 'Soumaya! They're shelling!
They're shelling! Get back!' She squeezes past them, searching
frantically for her father.*

A car came to a sudden stop just inches away from him,
but he stood unharmed and expressionless, staring into the
distance. The children on the green lawn giggled, and the
twisted vines around the brick walls and all the sights and

sounds he once knew filled his senses. He smiled serenely.

Soumaya took his arm gently, led him away from the crowd, back to the comforting safety of their apartment. As always, he didn't see her. She followed his eyes as they focused on the rubble on the other side of the street. This was what it had now become, nothing but shattered glass, wild weeds choking the grounds and climbing up the crumbling blackened walls. Yet underneath this sad exterior a shadow of the school's former glory was still present in the simple rooms, the crumbling wooden doorway below the red tiled roof and the elegant stone columns at the entrance.

All this captivated him so. Yet for Soumaya it was nothing but a sad reminder of a lost life, a memento best left buried under the rubble.

JANA FAOUR

Not Today

The ball flew high up into the clouds and landed out of sight. It's probably on the steps behind the trees, I thought. Suad and I ran up to get it. Sure enough, there it was, on the second step of the winding staircase. Suad ran and picked it up. She was always faster than I was. I followed her back to the playground. Suddenly she stopped and stared at me.

'Are you Muslim or Christian?' she asked.

'What's a Muslim?'

'It means you believe in Muhammad.'

'My dad's name is Muhammad,' I replied. But because my uncle's name is also Muhammad, I wondered which one she meant.

'So what are you?'

'I don't know!' I yelled.

'How can you not know?'

Suad has been my friend for a long time. We do everything together. 'What are you?' I asked.

'Muslim.'

'Then, so am I.'

'Good. Let's play.'

Suad was positioning the ball for another kick when the bell rang. We rushed to the old school building to get our stuff. As I packed my schoolbag I wondered whether mummy or daddy would pick me up today. My mum was at the door waiting. Normally I'd run to her for the customary hug and kiss. Not today though. I couldn't wait to give her my bag, which seemed heavier than usual. She gently placed my backpack over her shoulder and we walked towards the dreaded staircase. As always I got up on the ledge and drifted into my fantasy world where the mud beneath the ledge was treacherous quicksand. In this fantasy world balance must be maintained no matter what.

As usual mum asked me about my day. I loved to tell her about it because she always listened enthusiastically. Not today though. I just didn't feel like it.

We finally reached the last step. Every day we stop here to catch our breath. Most of the other kids and their mums do too. This is the spot where the mums meet and talk. Sure enough, Suad and her mum were waiting. The mums greeted one another and chitchatted. Usually, I'd take advantage of this opportunity to jump around in the puddles of rainwater with Suad. Not today though. Today there would be no jumping in puddles.

Saud's mum was a big lady. She talked very, very slowly. With her white hair and big glasses she didn't look very much like all the other mums. In fact she didn't look like a mum at all but I didn't tell Suad that. I didn't want to make her cry.

Suddenly the sky lit up. My mum and I ran towards the gate. We had to get home before it started to rain. We walked past the bakery. The sweet smell of hot bread lured me inside every time. Not today though. I just wanted to get home.

The moment mum opened the front door I rushed in to get

ready for lunch. I was already sitting at the dining room table when she came in with my soup bowl. I was deep in thought: does mummy know if we're Muslim? Of course she does. Mummy knows everything. When she finally placed the hot bowl in front of me, I asked her. I couldn't wait anymore. I had to know.

'Mum. Are we Muslim?'

She turned around, shocked.

'Why do you want to know?'

Her avoidance annoyed me.

'I want to know. Are we?'

Hesitantly, she answered. 'Yes, but it shouldn't matter to anyone but you.' Her words after that just faded into the background like a soft hymn as she patiently explained what it meant. Mummy warned me that, if anyone asks, I shouldn't tell. It was no one's business but my own. She spoke angrily about how so many people do bad things to good people just because they're different. I didn't understand everything she said, but I could see that those people made mummy really angry. That day I knew I never wanted to be like them.

Mum talked and I listened. Now, thirteen years later, I can still hear her words.

Suad continues to be a good friend. Neither she nor I ever talk about that conversation we had so long ago. I'm pretty certain she does not recall it. But I do. Although Suad did not grow up to be the sectarian fanatic one might have imagined she would become, I sometimes wonder whether things would have been different between us if my reply had been different.

When I think back to that cold, rainy day, a day I shall never forget, I feel no anger or hatred only sadness, the sadness that comes with the mature knowledge of life's grave imperfections. On that day a little girl's innocence faded. She was robbed of the bliss of ignorance. Her tiny shoulders carried the burden of a nation's prejudices. Still, as the little girl matured, she tried to follow her mother's advice – not to judge people by their religion – but as her shoulders grew wider and stronger the burden grew too. On that day a little girl discovered that there were walls in her playground and that, no matter how hard she tries, there are some she may never be able to tear down.

Maybe mum doesn't know everything after all!

MAI GHOUSSOUB

Red Lips

I was once involved in building an installation on the theme of refugees. One part of the installation consisted of objects that could be easily carried along if one had to leave home and venture into an unknown future with little or no warning. The objects sent to the artists were mainly memories of survival: keys, deeds, diplomas, radios and purses. Only one item defied what seemed essential for a future of migration into the unknown – a tube of red lipstick. To me this did not seem like a light and superfluous item to take. I understood immediately the source of the sender's survival reflex. She – for it can only be a woman or a man who feels like a woman – was ready to journey along a dark road carrying a strong message of life and defiant energy. I understood because of the red lipstick marks that still haunt a corner of my memory, hidden like an explosive dream in a now abandoned convent that once stood discreetly on a hill, high up in the Lebanese mountains.

I was a teenager preparing for the baccalaureate exam with my friends Nada and Joumana when we decided on a tranquil location that was ideal for concentration. Silence and a long distance from the city and its attractions became crucial for our studious goal. A secluded convent run by Italian nuns for novices seemed perfect: it removed us from the presence of males for two weeks. '*Retraite*' was the word we used in those days – retreating, withdrawing from ordinary life, from our routine, but mainly from the lightness of normal being.

The convent was hauntingly silent. We learned from a somewhat less rigorous Italian nun that the order was hosting very young girls from 'respectable families' whose fortunes had known better times and who, for lack of a dowry, were unmarriageable. A convent was the most suitable alternative for these would-be spinsters, especially this one, where only girls from '*bonnes familles*' were admitted. The deadly silence that surrounded us was eerie, thanks to the binding oath made by every newcomer ('a privileged girl' as our nun put it) to be mute for six months. The few Italian nuns who ran the place spoke as little and as softly as possible out of respect for the novices' vow and out of love for 'the tears of Mary and the suffering of her son, Jesus Christ'.

There were dozens of novices, rushing silently through the dark corridors. We met them briefly on our way to the dining room, and our curious eyes searched eagerly for their faces, but they always managed to escape our gaze. Their eyes avoided us, fixing incessantly on the tiled floor whenever they passed us. Their bodies looked small and fragile under their neat black tunics. Only the Mother Superior appeared tall and upright in this convent. Her instructions, on the first day of our retreat, were uttered through thin lips that were as stiff as the rules that presided over the lives of this community of secluded and hushed women.

We were scheduled to spend two weeks in this haven of

perfect isolation, but on the seventh day the scene that recurs like a dark red dream in my sleepless nights turned the convent into disarray, cutting short our worthy and scholarly endeavour. It is because of this scene, on the seventh day in this remote convent, that I understand how a refugee can proudly hold a lipstick tube in the face of a threatening future.

> *Red is the Absolute: it is pure. Its dazzling power*
> *Stands for the warmth of the sun and the mystery of life.*
> *Red is transgression. Red is energy.*

The Mother Superior's lips loosened into a delighted smile when she informed us that today was the Pope's feast day and that the novices would be allowed to roam freely around the convent, to enjoy themselves any way they saw fit as long as the vow of silence was respected. Soon a few novices stood near the door of the large room that Nada, Joumana and I were sharing. Their steps, at first timid and hesitant, became more assertive upon our insistent hospitality. They were obviously amazed by our messy and overcrowded room, but their faces turned crimson and more candid when Nada produced a large tin full of biscuits. They suppressed their giggles, hiding their mouths with their hands, as Nada battled with layers of clothes and books, mingled with some make-up kits, to free a box packed with sweets and chocolates. A bullet-like stick fell out, rolling noisily on the bare floor. Joumana picked it up and moved towards the mirror. She could never resist lipstick: she pulled off its golden cover, revealing a glittering magenta that she spread magnificently over her stretched lips.

> *Since ancient Egyptian times, women have been staining their lips*
> *with everything from berry juice to henna, from a paste made of*
> *crushed red rocks to the combo of wax. The ancient Egyptians*

went to their graves with rouged lips.

I do not have a clear memory of how it all started. All I can see now is a room turned upside down by a bewildering frenzy. The novices were smearing their faces with all the lipstick the three of us had brought: they took hold of our make-up kits like famished birds of prey competing for their victims. They snatched them from each other, looking for more under the sheets, behind the books, under the tables. Red, cherry red, mulberry, burgundy paste everywhere, all over the novices' lips. Red like cranberry juice, like deep wounds. Graffiti red, dark orange patches over white skin and pale necks. Soon the novices started exchanging shades of red, rushing back and forth to the mirror, looking victoriously at their own reflection, tearing off their veils and collars, revealing shaved and patchy skulls, wiping off the spots they had kissed over and over again on the mirror to make new space for lip-marks, for the fresh red stains on the mirror's surface.

Red is the colour of fire and blood. It is the fire that burns inside the individual. Below the green of the Earth's surface and the blackness of the soil lies the redness, pre-eminently holy and secret. It is the colour of the soul, the libido and the heart. It is the colour of esoteric lore, forbidden to the uninitiated.

A novice, short and wilful-looking with her flushed baby face, went into wild, intoxicating motions. She kept bending her torso, throwing her shaved head downwards, springing her body upright and flinging her arms in all directions. She seemed to perform an angry and disconnected ritualised dance, oblivious of the uproar and chaos surrounding her. Noises emerged from the red faces that twirled and rushed around, filling the room with a buzzing mad clatter. Sounds like shrieking laughter came out of red candy throats and brown glittering tongues. Screams like those of warriors seeking a desperate victory emerged from the now revealed and shaved heads of the frantic novices. Some had patches of hair scattered over their skull like badly tended lawns. I suddenly realised that more novices had joined in the frenzied feast, turning our room into a frightening maze of violet and wine-dark surfaces.

> *Red embodies the ardour and enthusiasm of youth. It is the colour of blood, the heat of the temper. It gives energy to excitement and to inflamed physical conditions. With its warlike symbolism, red will always be the spoils of war or of the dialectic between Heaven and Earth. It is the colour of Dionysus, the liberator and orgiastic.*

The tall and dark figure of the Mother Superior loomed before us, putting a sudden end to the uncontrollable madness in the room. She must have stood there, unnoticed, for a while before silence fell upon our room that now looked like an abandoned and desolate battlefield. It was a heavy and long silence that emphasised the languid embrace of two novices oblivious to the sudden change of mood around them. With her eyes half closed, her head leaning on the wall, one of the two was lustfully offering her neck, smeared with red lip marks, to the passionate kisses of the other.

Rage like red burning arrows tensed the lips of the Mother Superior, intensifying the paleness of her complexion. She appeared like a colourless mask strapped inside her black tunic, as rigid as a tightrope-walker immobilised in a snapshot.

'Stop it!' she finally managed to scream. Her cry had the effect of a slap hitting the two novices on the face. They disentangled their bodies furtively and rushed out of the room.

Red is the colour of the heart. Red is forbidden, free, impulsive. Red roses like the petals of desire. Did you know that in the 1700s the British Parliament passed a law condemning lipstick? It stated that women found guilty of seducing men into matrimony by cosmetic means could be tried for witchcraft. How was this law received in the red light district?

Her words resonated sharply in the silent room. She was like a general summoning a fallen army on a desolate and chaotic battlefield. The novice, who was dancing and spinning like a drunken scarecrow was now lying on the floor, smiling through her half-opened lips – pink-purple lips – in a state of placid and satisfied detachment, while the Mother Superior stood like pure anger, controlled and obstinate.

Red is anger. Red warns, forbids and awakens vigilance. Red is blood, red is fire. Red like full-bodied wine is the devil's choice.

'Evil! Dirty! Evil!' The words emerged from the depth of her throat as if struggling to get through her thin lips. 'The devil has conquered your souls and your flesh. The wombs of your mothers have rejected you and you have fallen into a dark abyss. Shame, shame on you and on your families! Ugly girls! Your lips are scarlet like the sinner's lips. Jesus will not be sacrificed twice. You will not be saved. Your bad blood has pierced your skin and stained your tunics. You will burn in hell, in deep red flames. Only fire will cleanse your swollen lips and spoiled innocence.'

The Mother Superior's tongue was moving fast, spinning like a wounded snake inside her wax-pale face. She was shaking but remained upright, stiff and furious, exhorting the forces of evil that had bewitched her novices.

'Go back to your rooms and lock yourselves in. You have wounded Jesus Christ and desecrated his home.'

Nocturnal red is the colour of the fire that burns within the individual and the earth. It is the colour of the devil's laughter, of hell's flames. Red is revolt.

There was a war and the convent is no longer there. It is said that two of the novices stayed behind in a rented brick house not far from the abandoned convent. According to the villagers they live like hermits, except that their lips are always heavily painted with bright red lipstick.

Nadine Rachid Laure Touma

Red Car

Yes it's over ...

That smile that used to wait around the corner of the left turn before the mosque is gone.

It was put away in some tiny muscle now triggered only by a scent, not by a feeling.

The scent of talcum powder under sweaty armpits, or the scent of someone who wants to commit suicide.

It was a rainy summer evening.

Wet, I walked down the empty narrow streets from the university to my apartment.

Tiny drops of rain taking me as their shelter.

Me, the massive body, sheltering drops of rain.

Flowers huddling with dew.

We walked together, alone, creating an illusion of light.

As if I became more than one, more than me.

It was a warm rain carrying the taste of all the smells of daylight.

The taste of car exhaust mixed with a little boy's hand selling a gardenia necklace, topped with a delicious woman's French perfume wrapped in freshly baked thyme bread.

It was still there.

That same red car that stood like a statue on that corner.

On, but not moving. On for a very long time. On for a very long distance.

It was pouring.

I started running when one of the doors of the red car opened.

A hand signalled me in.

I went into the red car without thinking.

I just went in.

The car was still on and not moving.

I was in it and could not make out the face of that inviting hand.

The bored streetlights played games with me, creating a silhouette of long hair, big head, small nose, broad shoulders, an unlit cigarette and a running engine.

I am sorry for getting your car wet.

I was drying myself.

That hand handed me a handkerchief.

Thank you.

The handkerchief smelled of my grandmother's drawers.

A mixture of lavender and no light.

Strange that this smell would make its way from an earthy past through the city walls.

Even the sound that it made on my skin reminded me of my grandmother's little hands looking through her linen, sifting through her memories, bringing her mother's embroidered scarf to her face and taking in all the scents of many years of widowhood.

This handkerchief belonged to my grandmother.

I could hear our breaths.

There was a bird-feeder clinging to my window.

Perhaps it was waiting for a rebellious night bird courting its companion.

Dripping seeds overflowing, holding onto the glass, sliding one after the other in hectic lines, moving slowly to the gutter, or to the sole of someone's shoe, or to the beak of a lonely bird, or to grow somewhere.

I like the idea of these seeds growing somewhere.

Strange, a car window for hungry birds.

The hair was dividing the space between us.

The car was shaking from the heavy rain.

Are you waiting for someone?

I felt the drops of water running along my breast, resting in the ripples of my stomach only to continue their journey and curve around my crotch.

Their final destination.

Silence.

We just sat in that small red beating heart.

I felt that I was breathing through the tiny wind-chime, hanging from the rear-view mirror, twinkling humid notes.

You should call the wind-chime a breath-chime.

I could feel a smile crossing from one side of the hair border to the other.

I was not afraid of this stranger who seemed so familiar to me.

In the distance everything was blurry and wet.

The sound of falling rain was not the romantic one that we hear on tile, it was more like the sound of my mum pouring dirty washing water from the balcony into the street.

I hope I am not keeping you from going somewhere, as soon as it stops...

Where are you going?

I am going to my apartment. It is just around the corner...

I know.

Rainy silences.

I am sorry I can't drive you there. My car won't move. It just turns on.

I love the feeling of being wet without getting wet. When it rains at night, I sit in my car, turn it on and pretend to travel. I just sit.

I wait for the rain to give me the courage to pour myself like it does, to part with the travelling clouds forever.

I sit and wait for you to cross the street.

Silent smiles.

Do you know the 'I once' game?

No.

It's very easy. Each sentence has to begin with I once and the meaning of all the sentences has to connect in some way. It goes on until one of the players has nothing to say. You start.

I once forgot

I once found a tear

I once cut a cloud into pieces

I once set fire to a stream

I once killed myself

I once was a butterfly

I once jumped on a spring mattress

I once saw you crossing the street wearing a red dress and I have fallen in love with you ever since

I once believed you

I once waited for you to cross that street again to see you before I kill myself, but I fell asleep waiting for you and eleven o'clock the time of my death went by wearing red

A dry silence.

A fast car splashed the red statue on wheels, shattering our vision into miniature rain drawings.

Strange how the rain changes its mood so quickly.

I am going to walk home.

The three of us are wearing red tonight.

Goodnight.

That same hand stopped me.

Please stay with me tonight.

The shadow of the raindrops was running along my hands like the veins of an old person, drawn by light and erased by gravity. Seeping through the sound of silenced rain and smiles was the sound of Muslim evening prayers coming from the mosque's minaret just around the corner. It was one of the very few mosques left where the muezzin still prayed, not some tape recording plugged into a speaker, screaming its prayers out and scratching the listener's beliefs, plunging my neighbour into justified modernism whereby he would take a recorded prayer tape with him to work and play it on his walkman at the time of the noon prayer, because his work place is in the Christian part of the city. 'No mosques there,' he says, with a sweaty moustache, wearing his blue trainers and carrying his rolled prayer rug under his arm.

This is my father chanting. Isn't his voice beautiful? I wish he talked to me the way he talks to God.

That hand slipped into mine.

A silent fall leaf, breathing in the same heat, sweating to dissolve into my blood, leaving me no space to speak, to ask, to utter. I did not move. Why was I smiling?

Spend my last night with me.

To be asked to spend the last night of someone's life with them is as if they are already dead. A delicious butterfly that lands in my belly button the night of its ephemeral melting.

Gentle kisses were dropped in my palm. Secrets you whisper

to the night pillow right before you surrender to sleep.

I turned the car off.

The beautiful voice of the muezzin was relentless, as if he was savouring every verse, chewing every note, releasing light.

A warm tongue was rolling around my fingers, one by one, encircling them. A nebula. A luminous vapour glowing in the dark.

I could hear the fallen cigarette rolling gently between my feet.

Left right. Right left. Left right.

I rested my head on a soft, tender, warm belly.

I could trace with my lips the hairline leading to the pubic grove.

I dipped my mouth in a shy belly button and scooped out a rolled umbilical cord and chewed on all its innocent childhood. My eyes were now resting on a hard nipple, my nose teased by sweaty talc powder while my mouth was crossing the river of life.

Two lines of sensuous moisture met with two stitching lips, with two entangled tongues, with two beating breaths. We hummed mutely.

Our hands were clapping on skin, applauding our desire. Our eyes finally met. We both stopped and just looked at each other for the first time. We looked deeply into each other's eyes. I felt we had just met after a long forced separation without having ever met.

I have a key to the mosque, let's go up to the minaret and look at the wet city. Don't worry my father won't be there now.

I did not resist the offer.

I had always admired minarets and envied men for their easy access into such ethereal flying spaces. We walked out of the red car towards the mosque in complete silence. Hand in hand we crossed the wet streets, we went around the corner where the mosque laid, a reclining figure of a tired wave, an odalisque hand picking the stars. The door of the mosque cringed under the key, but then relaxed and opened up.

A smell of naphthalene rugs filled the darkness.

The outside lights seeped through the many small windows, tracing the travelling dust particles into beautifully intersecting lines.

We started twirling around the lines of dust.

Our laughter bounced off our shadows.

Our shadows bounced off our laughter.

The walls glided around us as if someone was drawing an endless curtain.

We fell on the rugs, dizzy, and just stayed there staring into the expanding ceiling.

Let's go up to the minaret.

We used a red torch that was inside a small cabinet. Tiny staircases. Winding around themselves. Unwinding to themselves. No end in sight. The sound of our footsteps resounded an echo of a distant marching band.

What if the entire city could hear us?

Dom tak dom dom tak tak tak.

Hand in hand we walked up and up and around and inside and up and around.

We stopped from time to time touching each other's faces as if to check that time hadn't left us there and walked away. I would like to imagine leaving time behind us but it scares me to think of time leaving us behind.

The stone was getting humid. I could feel the fresh air opening up.

Close your eyes and just follow my arms.

Held from the back I let myself be led to the sky.

Open your eyes
Only if you kiss me
Open your eyes
Only if you kiss me
Only if you kiss me
We kissed under moving clouds and erased stars.

I opened my eyes to a dripping city and to a woman wearing red, holding me tightly on the cliff of enchanted prayers.

We sat in the alcove of the minaret with our legs hanging in the vast city sky. I took her hand and traced with it the path that led me every day for the past month to the red car, to a destiny I would have never imagined.

A path that was as big as her hand.

We walked it with our fingers. We followed the streetlights and the corners. We stopped at the different military checkpoints. We crossed the streets and we met around the corner of the left turn before the mosque. We looked at each other. We smiled. We kissed endlessly.

She leaned over, gently took one of my red shoes off and whispered something in it.

Where is your favourite part of the city?

The sea.

My shoe was beautifully flying westward.

Look, a red shooting star.

I said with tears caught in my throat.

It flew so far.

I was sure I could hear it falling in the sea.

Now you know where to go every time you want to hear what I have whispered.

A red shoe was to become my anchor in a city of war with a seafront but no shore.

I was crying.

She was crying.

It was raining again.

Very warm and soft rain.

I started undressing her.

First the red shirt.

At every button she whispered a name or a place in my ear.

And between every button her tongue pierced the silence in my ear.

Maybe they are places she has loved, people she has met.

I bathed the red shirt in warm rain and pressed it against my face.

My red dress was twirling above the city. A red rain poppy.

Some things end before they begin.

And some things do not have a beginning but they never end.

Omega: Definitions

I am a Muslim feminist from the Fertile Crescent.

I have a tattoo on my right wrist.

It's of God.

I designed it.

Do you know where the Fertile Crescent is?

One day when we were alone together Shah treated me in a way I didn't like at all.

Shah means king in Persian.

I don't remember the details. But it was theatre.

I don't think it made any difference.

I don't usually talk about my religion.

Some Muslims might not accept me as one because I sometimes drink alcohol. I don't keep Ramadan because fasting makes me go hypo, I don't like polygamy, and also I don't believe in hell. Some Muslims might call me a renegade.

I don't accept the charge.

Islam means surrender.

I would like to make a pilgrimage to Mecca.

It was late spring. The gardenias outside had bloomed.

My fridge was filled with black cherries I had bought that day.

Back home when the gardenias come out they make garlands out of them and sell them in the streets. Some women wear them in their hair.

Everybody smells sweet and fresh.

My hair is too short for flowers. Too short for him to get a good grip on.

He grabbed the back of my neck.

Don't fight me so much.

Part jest, part force.

We met in a *Zawya*.

This is the Arabic word for the place where Sufis go to hold *Dhiker*.

Dhiker means remembrance, and it involves meditation and chanting. Sufism is nostalgia, the nostalgia of the heart and the anticipation of its homecoming.

The sweet, sweet journey home.

It was not a very orthodox *Zawya* and so men and women could sit and pray together.

Afterwards they serve baklava and mint tea. Some people smoke a cigarette outside.

Sufis practise Istislam. This takes you a level beyond surrender. It is inner submission, abandonment to His will. It is anatomy of the soul stuff.

I went to another, very orthodox *Zawya* in the suburbs of East London once. I met a couple there. He was from the Midwest of the United States somewhere and he had a long blond beard. He was dressed all in white. He spoke Arabic beautifully. I wondered how he had come across Islam.

Or indeed, Istislam.

She told me that they met in Jordan. She was dressed in black.

Some charismatic ascetic mystic had introduced them.

I caught myself thinking, I hope it was not Abu Musab al-Zarqawi.

I am sure you have heard of Abu Musab al-Zarqawi.

She was in a very strict *Hijab*.

Hijab means screen or curtain, but it is more commonly used to describe Muslim women's dress code.

The Koran itself is vague about how women should dress.

But you would never guess it from looking around you.

Inside the *Zawya* we sat on the floor.

I didn't like being separated from the men by a nylon curtain and having to whisper Ya Latif hundreds of times, while the men raised their voices. When you invoke God as Latif, with His grace you draw the divine quality of gentleness down to you, so it can touch the floor.

The men's chanting behind the curtain is vigorous, martial. They are soldiers, advancing towards God.

The subdued tones of the harem are more of a supplication. We are calling God to us.

The word harem can be used synonymously for women. It means that which is sanctified, forbidden.

A young woman who had come in the severest outfit, a black chador complete with gloves and face veil, was having some trouble keeping the volume down. American Sufi's wife looked at her reproachfully a few times.

Incidentally chador is a Persian word, not Arabic.

Different language, different civilisation.

Afterwards, when you finish chanting, you run your hands over your face once as though you were washing.

For more fervour, you can also run your hands once over your neck, chest, stomach and legs.

His name is spiritual water: you are clean.

The American Sufi's wife did this.

I wanted so much to belong.

I didn't ask for initiation.

The American Sufi told me afterwards that one day towards the end of 2001, someone found the mere sight of him so provocative they threw a take-away curry at him on the same train platform where the three of us were standing.

And presumably called him a terrorist bastard.

I didn't get initiated at the Persian *Zawya* where I met Shah either.

In Persian the word for *Zawya* is *Khanaga*.

In English you just say Sufi House.

Afterwards we walked along The Cut behind the South Bank and got something to eat.

I couldn't swallow any of my Turkish food.

I didn't like it anyway. Expensive hummus.

He talked about war, government and evolution.

He is quite Hobbesian.

I should have bolted like a colt on his first gallop.

On the way home I left my scarf and all the reading material I had picked up at the *Khanaga Zawya* Sufi House on the bus.

It was a Missoni scarf.

But don't let me get off track. The dark angel poured an exotic elixir, and I drank.

If a man thinks you are submissive, he will go weak at the knees. According to the tradition in which I was brought up, you must treat your man like a High Priest. Worship at the hem of his garment and wait for your reward. But there are a lot of charlatans out there, ready to take you for a spin. Especially if you are a woman on the constant verge of ecstatic adoration. In that case, then you must be a little vigilant, sweet thing.

Shah lowered his gaze, and whispered gently, I'd like to see you again.

Let's meet in the park. I'll need nature.

Let's meet after dark. I'll want walls.

When I'm in love I tend to act a little berserk.

I guess it's just how my love atoms are configured.

The berserkers were ferocious, superhuman Norse warriors who donned bearskins before battle.

I think Shah was a little berserk too.

In times of turmoil and times of plenty, I seek His guidance and Mercy.

Emmanuel, Buddha, and the Lion of Judah.

Hook me up with all of them.

But it was no good. I developed a cannibalistic intestinal craving for him.

Monastic consciousness remained far from my reach.

I reasoned: we speak a different language and come from different civilisations but we are both olive-skinned.

I don't think olive-skinned best describes the shade of colour of the skin of olive-skinned people.

There are black and green olives.

I prefer green ones because they are more bitter and biting.

I focus on this thought.

The modern *hijab* is the most sexually explicit piece of clothing there is.

I know this because every time I see a woman in one I have to restrain myself from running up to her and ripping it off.

That would take some doing.

Still, each to her own.

And despite everything, I sometimes wrap my own head in a scarf.

My urban turban.

For the summer I have one made of brilliant white cotton. It is embroidered with bright red and gold threads. I bought it in an Ethiopian shop near the tube station at Finsbury Park.

When I wear it I feel blessed but I don't wear it enough.

Some Rasta women wear this scarf.

I will tell you about Rasta another time.

Suffice it to say that it's a biogenic religion. Rastafari is never forgotten. He lives and He reigns.

It is an ubiquitarian kind of thing.

If you don't know what this is, look it up.

In the winter I tuck my hair under a long piece of red and black muslin.

I bought it from some nomadic women in the Syrian steppes. They wore it as a shawl that hung from their head all the way down the back of their bodies.

I'll never forget those undulating silhouettes.

I want to learn to ululate.

I notice that people look at me differently when I cover my hair.

They seem curious and more respectful.

Sometimes I wish I could rub the tattoo off my wrist.

But that's the kind of woman I am.

I play fast and loose and then regret it.

When I became annoyed with Shah he said he was just an Alpha male.

How else do I show you how much I like you, girl?

He seemed genuinely at a loss.

Sometimes, instead of girl, he said bitch.

I guess it's just the way his loving goes.

Alpha is, as we know, the first letter of the Greek alphabet.

It is based on the Alef, which was invented by the Phoenicians around 1200 BC, perhaps earlier.

It was August.

Figs were in season.

I like figs because it is the fruit which is the most delicate to eat.

Some Evangelical Christians associate the fig tree with prophecy, and signs of His coming. They are waiting remember, for the battle of Armageddon, the conversion of the Jews, and the saviour of all of humanity.

Or something like that.

Shah's aura is gloomy, even on a bright August afternoon.

Not that I can read auras but if I could I would have said his was inky.

So we were both olive-skinned and we were both Muslims.

Don't get that wrong, we are something very alien and very different from you.

Let me tell you something blood.

They know but don't tell.

Islam may have evolved as part of the Judeo-Christian tradition, but its roots are deliciously, rock-worshippingly pagan.

The supreme deity of the pre-Islamic Arabs was called Al-Lah.

Al-Lah was Lord of the Ka'bah and High God of Mecca.

He reigned with the help of a female trinity, His three daughters. Al-Lat the Goddess of Light and Fertility. Manat the Goddess of fate was represented by the dark phase of the moon. Uzza the patron Goddess of Mecca was associated with Venus, the morning star.

The crescent moon and star that represent Islam are reminiscent of this astral religion.

But the devil, as they say, is in the detail.

Some fundamentalist Christians use this as an argument to prove that Islam is equivalent to idolatry.

More accolades to Islam, I say.

Sometimes, people talk about British Muslims. If anyone ever called me a British Muslim to my face I would be tempted to bash them over the head because that is sloppy thinking.

But then I might come across a little hot.

A little hot-headed.

Which I'm not.

I don't like prototypes and I don't like racial profiling.

There is no such thing, sorry to break it to you, as a prototype British Muslim.

If you don't know, investigate.

Don't essentialise.

Stop looking for our chiefs.

I don't think 'Muslim feminist from the Fertile Crescent' best describes me.

The Fertile Crescent is an area that stretches from the eastern shore of the Mediterranean to the Persian Gulf. It includes ancient Mesopotamia, a.k.a. Iraq, where right now elite gangsters are filling up their piggy-bank with Straight Cold Theft.

My ancestors came to the Fertile Crescent from the Caucasus.

There is a place called Historic Palestine.

In my tradition we are honour-bound to entertain strangers, no questions asked.

Everybody's blood runs through my veins.

This makes me more white than you, more Christian than you, more Jewish than you.

E pluribus unum is one out of many, in Latin.

The spiritual path feels strained at times.

Shah is agonistic, vain.

The quality I deplore most in a man is vanity.

He plays at being an *Evolué* but he values violence.

He doesn't rate consent much, can live without the dialectic.

At most he will acknowledge that his needs are complex.

He laughs and jokes a lot.

His voice is deep and soft.

His eyes are brutal.

Where there is Alpha there is Omega.

That's underdogs on top, if you know your New Testament.

Your Matthew.

Your Book of Revelation.

I seek solace in the words of the Comforter.

I take solace wherever I can find it.

When people want to make sure you are not a terrorist, they make facile remarks such as 'surely you must agree with the broad principles of democracy'.

Yes and no.

I have heard it said it is the dictatorship of the majority.

But never mind that. It is as though they are looking for a fissure in your personality.

Don't let me remind you of what happened in New York.

Don't let me preach equality.

The 'suicide bombing' endemic pandemic has got to them.

And so you have to talk nice and prove you are not a terrorist sympathiser.

That you are no perpetrator, candidate.

Not a warmonger, death-peddler, hate-hawker.

A bit rich I think.

Anyway democracy is a Greek word.

And the Greeks kept slaves.

Come on, let us peruse the morning papers.

Seeing is believing.

Cruel and unjust regimes are allegedly falling like dominoes in my neck of the woods.

The last time I was in Beirut I took a walk to Martyrs'

Square.

Martyrs' Square has been renamed Democracy Square.

Forgive me if I can't join in with the buoyancy.

But I feel unrepresented.

A red and white Virgin Megastore in the background blends in with a sea of red and white flags in the foreground.

It provides a seamless visual continuum.

It's the ideological continuum I'm afraid of.

They're waiting for world peace to break out in Lebanon.

I reckon it's too late for that.

We are fully engaged. We are on high alert.

If you've ever been anywhere you'll know the scene.

Papers please. Open the boot.

But let me take the edge off that chill.

On clear evenings, as the light changes and before the sky slowly fills with stars, Venus, the planet second only to the sun, appears to usher in the dream-time.

On a warm, wild beach somewhere, south of here, crabs are crawling back into their holes.

Nature saying goodnight, it's been a pleasure doing it to you.

They know, but don't tell.

There is existential weight in loving.

Nature is the higher self.

His gentleness flows like a river through a mountain.

So bask in the presence of the blessing.

For whatever happens it is written that it was written.

Maktoub.

HOUDA KARIM

A Slice of Beach

Trapped, I'm trapped. Night and day I wait for him, hoping to see him on the shore of this turquoise beach, hoping that our meeting will restore my tranquillity. I try to escape my feelings by looking at the children, but I know they find me effeminate. My oracle goddess no longer focuses her sad eyes on me.

The children followed me, whispering to each other and pointing at me.

'Listen you street fag, don't stay here. Go away or else we'll throw stones at you.'

'Stop! He is Loulwa's brother! Don't say another word. She defends him all the time. She might not let us work anymore.'

'Work? Work as what?' I ask.

'It's none of your business. Go away! It's our work, all of us. Go screw yourself. Anyway, here comes your boyfriend.'

That's when I saw his car. The face came nearer, the eyes spoke of love and tenderness. I drifted over to him. Suddenly life became beautiful, the atmosphere pleasant. I took a deep breath out of pleasure, out of the desire to be with him.

Loulwa came nearer. She wanted to take me away.

'I'm coming with you, I'm following you,' I said to him very quickly so that no obstacle would come between us. He placed his hand on Loulwa's shoulder affectionately: 'Come with us. We're going for a ride. I only have this sports car for a few hours. We're going to have lots of fun.'

Deafening music, intoxicating smiles, the handkerchief flying in the wind. Too much happiness all at once! Our laughs merge. His body is near mine.

Loulwa wants to eat.

'I'm inviting you to a classy restaurant for some delicious fish.'

'Do you have enough money to invite us for lunch?'

'I have the cash. It's up to you to find the best restaurant.'

'The one I've heard of is "The Fisherman" in Jbeil. It should do. Let's go and see posh people. I want to see posh people.' He broke into laughter. My sister amused him.

'Easy thing, posh people! I'll show them to you tonight,' he said.

'Do you know any? Yassine told me about them. He was performing during one of their private functions and was very impressed. And how come you know such people?'

'How do you think I manage to drive a car like this? It costs a fortune. It belongs to some rich people who own three cars.'

'You must be kidding. I don't believe you.'

'You'll see what I mean with your own eyes.'

All my senses were awakened as I listened to the conversation. God, how good I felt, as his hand gently caressed my shoulder while the other expertly manoeuvred the steering wheel. God, how happy we were!

Translated by Sleiman El-Hajj

A Pomegranate Notebook

The cold uncaring winds of March blew the bride's white veil. At first, it rained hard but then the rain turned soft and light. The donkey, with its red saddle and the carnations around its neck, walked slowly as if it knew its burden that day was one of happiness. Helena, the young bride, was seated on the donkey, trying to protect her adornments with the umbrella of her uncle, the priest. Her heart was heavy with sadness, and her mind, with a sort of worried surrender, tried to keep up with the events of the day.

The choice of Said as a husband for Helena made her mother happy. Helena herself had had no say in the matter; for how could a pure girl choose her own husband? Said's resounding footsteps had created fear in her heart and the hearts of her girlfriends whenever he passed by their playground. She never told anyone of this fear, but she immediately felt it whenever she saw him approaching. She would hear his sonorous voice before catching sight of his moustache that curved upwards towards his temples and his whip that lashed against his leather boots. Helena always hid when he stormed by, waiting for the tree branches to settle.

Her heavy heart leaped out of her chest the day her mother told her, with some pride, that it was Said's mother who had decided to make Helena the wife of her eldest son.

'Mother, this man scares me. His footsteps sound like a regiment of soldiers,' Helena told her mother.

But her mother's only concern was that the neighbours might hear her objection.

'Don't you dare repeat this outside the house. Said will become your husband and you will soon love his footsteps. They are the footsteps of a strong man, unlike those of that Chahine who moves around like a jar of oil.'

Helena sighed and was quiet. There was no use objecting: her mother had given Said's mother a promise, and it was improper to break a promise. She would move out of her mother's house, that loving but broken woman, and into Zmurrod's house, the woman whose reputation shook the walls of the neighbourhood. She was a woman in the fullest sense of the word. In fact very few women were like her. Zmurrod brought up her children single-handedly after her husband's death. She was also a pious woman, and a skilled midwife who had delivered many male children. It was evident that Zmurrod was a woman with a strong mind, for all the village women came to her for advice: she was their reference in all matters.

In the hope of easing her gloomy heart, Helena kept repeating to herself all the compliments the women in the village heaped on Said's mother.

'With her you will live safely, Helena. And who knows, you might even learn from her how to become a professional mourner in the surrounding villages. What better calling is there to help the soul return to its Maker?'

Helena remembered her uncle's funeral. She was seven then

and it was the first time she had been allowed to approach a deathbed. Her uncle lay on embroidered sheets and Zmurrod was leaning over him, describing him in so many wonderful words, words he had certainly never heard when he was alive. Zmurrod stayed by his deathbed and did not leave until he was taken for burial. Her trembling voice had a great effect on the mourners and those offering condolences. It was an invitation to weep but it also had the power to console those grieving.

Helena remembered how her aunt used to insult her uncle. She would curse him, accusing him of being lazy, slow, irresponsible and cowardly. Yet in death, Zmurrod called him a brave knight, although he had ridden nothing more than his donkey to and from the mill. Helena remembered his patched trousers, but Zmurrod said he wore a silk cloak embroidered with gold.

The seven-year old girl thought that perhaps these words of reverence and glorification were a magic elixir that would change the dead person's mind about departing from the world. As she recalled this scene, the energy flowed through her veins again, for she secretly hoped she would inherit the gift of mourning from this strong woman. Perhaps, like Zmurrod, she would be able to change reality, erase poverty and humiliation with glorious rhymes, erase the sins of the villagers, and send them to their God as pure, rich heroes.

The beast hurried down the slope, while under his hoofs drifted streams of mud and hard stones. A strong wind blew out of nowhere as they approached the groom's village: it took hold of the white veil and blew it off the bride's head and into the distance. The guests who were accompanying the bride on foot paused to discuss what to do. They separated into groups and followed the direction of the wind, searching for the veil among the blueberry bushes. According to tradition, a bride with no veil is a bad omen. Helena's grandmother told her that a bride who got married hastily or eloped ended up a widow. Helena saw her mother in the distance waving the now wet and torn veil in the air: 'We found it hanging on a blueberry branch. The wind has torn it to shreds. What a shame!' She immediately ordered her nephew to go to the convent and rent a veil from the nuns at any cost. The bride must not enter her groom's home bareheaded.

On that March day Helena sensed the hardships that awaited her. Early that morning her mother had been proud and happy as she prepared for the days to come: 'Tomorrow Helena will send us a supply of soap and oil.' However, now she felt her mother's unease. The events of the day had gone contrary to her expectations. Strangely, only Helena remained unaffected, for she had given in to her fate. It was as if she had joined the guests but had nothing to do with the wedding itself. Until that day, she had known nothing of the world except for her house and neighbourhood. Her mother even thought that playing with the neighbourhood children was a waste of time, a sign of irresponsibility. So she gave Helena things to do all day long: 'Helena, bathe your brothers and sisters... Helena, sort the lentils... Helena, shell the peas ... Helena, feed the chickens... Helena, milk the goat...' Helena was so busy that she never had time to look at herself in the mirror. She had no idea that her eyes were the colour of leaves and that her brown face was round like the full moon. She grew up in poverty, without any education, without a black school uniform, and without a school bag full of dreams. Early on in her life she went to the field with her sisters to feed the cows and harvest the crop. Her mother taught her how to breed silkworms. Their prayers and vows were the size of mountains, but their faith brought little money. Despite their poverty Helena's mother bought her daughter a piece of white silk cloth and had it made into a wedding dress in the neighbouring village: she did not want Helena's new family to think they were poor or miserly.

On her wedding day Helena was allowed to look at herself properly in the mirror for the first time and was surprised to see a beautiful young girl dressed in white staring back at her.

The day after the wedding the bashful bride accompanied her husband and his mother to the city to buy a wedding ring, necklace and clothes. Once they returned home, Helena was amazed at how Zmurrod ordered her son around. Ironically, the man who had terrified her with his footsteps was scared of his mother and a slave to her every whim.

Translated by Mirna Haykal

JOCELYN AWAD

Khamsin

When Manal was born, the elders' verdict was devastating: her previous life would have enormous bearing on her destiny. She would have to live with an infirmity, the dead weight of mistakes she would never remember making. They agreed that for God's will to be observed, no effort would be made to cure her infirmity. They spoke of resignation, the only virtue they deemed possible in the face of such a cruel fate.

The wind blew from nowhere, regaining its course after a brief pause. Unrelentingly it swept across the Druze Mountain and the neighbouring regions: the Golan that extended to the west and the Ledja to the northwest, with its immense reddish lava.

On this November morning the wind aggressively attacked the volcanic mass, tearing off large blocks that went flying into the desert region of southern Syria.

The wind that wondered in the fields of wheat during the summer months suddenly awoke from a long seasonal rest and established itself as lord and master of the plateau.

It rushed softly into the Bedouin tents, making the goatskins flap, and when evening fell it inflated the earth-red tunics of the peasants whose shifting silhouettes as they returned home from the fields moved against a blazing sky.

However, its real anger and fury fell right above the Soueida town centre, in the heart of the Druze Mountain. Here it sent swirls of volcanic dust and hurled them at the enclosures made of brown stone stolen from the Byzantine churches of long ago. Sand stuck to the walls and seeped into the cracks of low doors and under the arches of the old Khan. Time and time again the wind thought it had buried it for good, but the relics remained obstinate and defiant, refusing to stay buried under the sand.

Chams left Soueida and made her way along the west road. Her will alone guided her body as she bent over to resist the wind. A sudden pain flashed through her back before travelling in dull waves to the rest of her body.

'God help me. The child is going to be born,' she whispered. Alarmed and panting, she paused for a moment to pray. She knew that Bedouin women often gave birth alone in the wilderness, cutting their baby's umbilical cord with sharp rocks. But this birth would be different, dangerous. She had felt this during the early months of her pregnancy, and now she was afraid of dying alone.

Chams walked faster. Her breathing was short and fast: she forced herself not to think of what was happening inside her body. The corner of her veil that pressed against her mouth, covering her head and eyebrows, offered no protection against the burning sand the wind threw in her face. The heavy, dark sky would soon release a torrent of rain. Chams had to make haste. She must reach the village. The pain came again, stronger and more precise. She clenched her fists and waited for it to ease. Suddenly her surroundings seemed hostile. The grey trunks of a few fig trees loomed against the lower end of the fields, and vines, as black and dry as her fears, snaked along the ground above her.

Finally the beams and dirt roof of her house came into view. An old woman stood at the entrance, her dress flapping wildly in the wind. Chams knew she was waiting for her because the old woman could predict events in advance. When she caught sight of Chams she stretched up her black silhouette and shouted a few words that were carried by the wind. Despite her exhaustion, Chams ran the remaining distance that separated them. 'Hurry Khalte, tell Amar the baby is coming!' Chams unrolled her mattress and threw herself on it. The pain assailed her brutally.

'This time I will not make it! Rabbi I can feel it! This child will be the death of me!'

There had been strange signs throughout. At first, they seemed of no importance, nothing but the same discomfort she had encountered during earlier pregnancies. It was the inability to function properly that began to startle her. She would break a dish, spill oil or salt, which, according to village tradition, were bad omens. At first she did not understand why this child tired her so much or why it kept kicking and moving around in her stomach for hours on end. Chams lost her touch, her green thumb: plants died when she touched them. But her fears reached a climax the night a messenger came from Bosra-Cham to inform her that her father was dying. Chams was squatting behind her wooden house cooking sour goat milk: her thighs were open and her stomach protruded. Her mother-in-law was hovering around like an old crow. Chams had to see her father, but she wondered if it was prudent to go when she was so close to giving birth. When her mother-in-law began to fuss and complain angrily, Chams immediately made up her mind.

'I will go... Allah will help me!'

The old woman persisted: she shook her head and insisted there would be complications. The child should have been born before the coming of winter and the delay was definitely a bad sign. Then, all of a sudden, her whining stopped. Chams paused at the doorstep and turned back, curious to know what had silenced her mother-in-law. The old woman was staring at the contents in the pot. With a heavy heart, Chams realised the milk had curdled. Chunks were floating on the surface. This was a sign that could not be misunderstood. She listened to the old woman say what she already knew: bad omens were associated with the coming of this child. Chams poured the bad milk over the thorn bushes and threw her worn-out shoe at the old woman, who scurried off yelling insults.

Chams reached Soueida and took the evening bus to Bosra-Cham, but when she arrived at her father's house, he had already passed away. She was assured that Allah, in taking his life, had relieved him of all his suffering. His liberated soul had already entered the body of a newborn child in the region. The women, dressed in black with white veils on their heads, were making preparations to spend a sad night with his widow. Their wails would continue until dawn. In the morning, despite her grief and exhaustion, Chams knew she had to make her way back quickly. She bid farewell to her grieving mother, who looked like a frozen statue, her face completely covered with the opaque veil widows wore.

As Chams waited for the bus that would take her back to Soueida, pain shot through her body and she could taste death on her lips. 'Rabbi, be merciful. I do not want to die like a dog on the road.'

As soon as she caught sight of Chams, her mother-in-law ran across the field oblivious to the sharp stones tearing at her bare feet. Excitement gave wings to her old age. Although Bou Hassan understood what was happening, he finished loading all the wood onto the back of his mule before he went to meet her. An icy wind, already wet, was blowing fiercely. Now his mother was yelling, screaming in his ear.

'Go quickly, my son. Fetch the midwife. Your wife is not doing well, and we fear for her life.'

Bou Hassan was upset: his wife had chosen her moment badly. He took his time stacking the wood in a dry place before mounting his beast. He was not moved by what his mother told him. Why should he be? Nothing tied him to the mother of his children any longer. The inhabitants of this rough area never fell prey to their feelings once the honeymoon was over. In fact a wife was more easily replaceable than a farm animal. However, he realised that Chams was strong and hardworking. Besides, the children were still very young. He preferred she not die. He dug his heels into the animal's side, and the beast darted off like an arrow against the wind.

Chams's mother-in-law returned to the house as fast as she could. Misfortune filled her with a strange kind of joy. After all, she must not miss out on the action. 'As God is my witness, I saw this coming,' she kept repeating to herself.

Chams's screams reached her ears long before she arrived. She found her sitting on a goatskin mattress, as was the tradition.

'Here my child,' said the old lady, giving Chams a ragged shirt. 'Tear it with your teeth whenever the contractions occur. It helps.'

To keep the children quiet they were sent away with their pockets full of nuts and dried raisins while the women gathered at the entrance of the house.

Amar, the most experienced of the women, had assisted in the delivery of the older children and was, in normal circumstances, extremely capable. But this birth was different. It was not going well: the baby was coming into the world in an abnormal manner. In fact it was not coming out at all. It was trapped inside Chams, who was growing weaker by the minute.

'*Ya Berri!*'

'If the *dayé* does not come, I will have the death of this woman on my conscience.'

Then Chams let out a cry like that of a wounded beast, which every man and woman in the village heard.

'*Ya Berri!*' moaned Amar. 'The feet aren't supposed to come out first.'

The old woman came closer to her daughter-in-law. One glance at Chams made her shiver to the bones. 'A monster! A monster is born into our family ... *Agibeh! Agibeh!*' the old woman screamed.

When the *dayé* finally arrived, she pushed aside the group of excited women and ordered the old woman who was still lamenting at the doorstep to shut up. She knew it would be a difficult birth, but there was urgency in the matter. Rolling her sleeves up, she knelt beside the young woman. Her skilful movements brought life back to Cham's body.

'Get me some hot bread,' she demanded when the delivery was finally completed.

The wheat bread, as soft as a wet towel, was useful in animating the newborn baby. A few taps against her face, chest and legs with the bread enabled the little girl to let out her first cry. The midwife recited the traditional incantations. The child was alive and so was the mother, but the *dayé* knew it would have been better had the baby died because it was obvious from the deformity in her legs that she would never walk.

Translated by Mirna Hakal

Zalfa Feghali

Wild Child

She had stayed with him in the hospital the night it happened, desperately clutching his lifeless body, willing his lungs to breathe, his heart to beat, willing him to come back to her. As dawn approached, she tried to piece together a day in her life without him. It was empty, blank and numb. Replaying the last thing he had said to her over and over again was not wise, but the words had taken on a life of their own – they floated around in her head and slid off the walls of her mind. The steps of her thoughts were littered with Dalí-esque versions of the sentence, 'I'm not here anymore.'

Nour's throat had been raw for the past two days: when she spoke, her voice sounded raspy and evil. She knew why, of course, everyone knew why. Her throat was raw from wailing at his funeral. Funerals have a nasty habit of doing that to a throat. But she wasn't particularly focused on her throat. She was more concerned about the last time she had seen Jihad because the fingernail that was on the middle finger of his left hand was missing.

The flowers, they decided, had to be blue. Ideally, of course, they should have been a warm pink because pink was his favourite colour. But to them pink was a womanly colour. Blue would just have to do. So blue it was, and the specially ordered irises were delivered on the day with just one hitch: they were far too happy-looking. In compliance with the men's orders, they were carefully carried to the roof by the servants and set in the sun to wilt.

The food had also caused some friction. One uncle argued that there should be no food at funerals, but his suggestion was dismissed after several stubborn and rather tough-looking aunts protested, insisting that death was a celebration and food had to be served. You see, it was a matter of honour.

Nour sobbed quietly in the corner of her room, her knees drawn up to her chest, her face in her hands.

They decided that *mansef* would be ideal.

The flowers were brought down from the roof, wilted and dry. Proud of their achievement, the men simply ordered the bouquets to be hung on the hooks that had been hammered into the wall the day before. Ever so gently, Nour, with the very tips of her fingers, touched a petal that was so dry it had become almost transparent. As soon as her fingers made contact with the petal, it disintegrated and disappeared.

Her first reaction was to kill herself, too. She expected his family to anticipate this and was extremely surprised when she realised their indifference to her, the ever-unwelcome daughter or sister-in-law. She soon saw that she meant nothing to them, even less than before. She was simply an obstacle, a wild child blocking their way to a life of complete honour.

She had dishonoured them when she had remained with his body the night of his death. She knew from the way they looked at her and whispered to each other that she was being blamed for the manner in which he had died, for his suicide.

After the funeral was over they had driven her to her brother's house. There was no need to live with them anymore. Her brother Khaled and his family had welcomed her warmly, as if to say that they understood. But she was oblivious to their warmth and care. It meant nothing to her. She was a phantom of desperation, invisible even to herself. Her slow descent into apparent madness pushed away all the people who loved her. They began to forget that she actually lived with them. Her room became a box, her prison and her sanctuary – away from accusing eyes, or even worse, away from pitying looks.

Khaled gave his sister her old bedroom, hoping that the sense of familiarity would help her overcome her grief. And for a short time it looked as if she was beginning to show a slight sense of normality. But, as time passed, Nour became thinner and paler, and even quieter than before. She was so withdrawn that the family grew accustomed to not seeing her for days at a time. When they did, the experience was more like an encounter with a ghost than with a human being.

Nour began to notice that whenever she ventured into parts of the house that her brother and his family frequented they would barely acknowledge her presence, even to the point of ignoring her. She had become a burden to them, a constant reminder that a stranger was in the house.

One night, months later, as Nour lay in bed, grief began to talk to her, whispering quietly into her right ear, 'I'm not here anymore.' Nour tried to ignore Grief, but the whispers grew louder, so loud that the voice seemed to be coming from inside her own head.

She looked down at her left breast. Mildly surprised, she realised that it was no longer there. She shifted her eyes to her right breast – it too had disappeared. Nour lifted her hand to feel her chest and realised that although she could feel her hands, they were nowhere to be seen.

For some reason this struck her as somewhat amusing. For the first time in months she smiled and wondered, although she could feel them, whether her lips and the tiny lines of blood that were now forming on them were actually there at all.

Nour decided that some experimentation was in order. She wiggled her toes (something of an inside joke between her and Jihad), and felt them. She knocked her heels together, and felt that too. Then, crunching herself up into the all-too familiar fetal position, she realised she could feel her shins, calves, knees and thighs. For a moment, Nour thought she heard laughter somewhere in the bedroom and realised that it was her own. She was laughing at the idea of being able to feel her body while it was invisible to the naked eye. But this possibility soon gave way to panic because her logic was telling her that what was happening was impossible. She pulled herself up and sat with her back against the headboard.

Nour woke up in that position. The sun was streaming in through the window, illuminating the room. Miniscule particles of dust were floating around, rearranging themselves for the day. She decided that it probably would not be the worst idea in the world if she rearranged herself too.

The sun was warming the skin on her knees, making them feel itchy. She reached down to scratch one knee and caught sight of nothing. The memory of the night before crept back into her thoughts. And then she made the connection, smiling as it came to her. 'I'm not here anymore.' Suddenly Grief was shouting, urging her over and over to do it.

She realised that the time was now. It was all over and she had to act before she lost complete control of herself. Nour ripped off the bed sheets and tied one of them to an iron rod near the window, carefully making a noose, with her trembling hands. Slowly, methodically, standing on a chair and pulling the noose around her neck, she cast one final look at the ever-present photograph of Jihad. And the wild child whispered: 'I'm coming.'

Trapped

She hated them all. She hated everyone she could think of, members of her own family, members of his family, and all their friends, old and new. This also included those who left and those who, like her, stayed and remained huddled in a corner, waiting. She even tried to remember the people she had forgotten, so she could hate them too.

She was at a loss as to how to express her all-consuming and comprehensive hatred until she decided to ignore her domestic chores by not hanging up the clothes thrown on the beds, and not even making up the beds. Then she thought about the dirty lunch dishes in the sink and decided to leave them there. Today she would not even clean the bathroom.

She sat on the two-seater in her usual corner, propped her feet up on the table and immediately felt a delicious lightness enter her body, almost like tranquillity: oh yes, she hated them all.

She felt eyes staring at her nasty, tranquil smile and glanced self-consciously at the opposite balcony. The neighbour on the second floor was hanging white, squeaky-clean washing on the line that stretched across her balcony. The man, with the grey moustache, was sitting in his usual place trying to focus his eyes on her face or on her outstretched legs. So she got up and carried the small wooden coffee tray and cigarettes to the bedroom. This quiet, faded place was ideal for focusing on hatred. The tray settled unevenly on the crumpled sheets, spilling the leftover coffee. But, although this made her laugh, she reached for a paper napkin from the box on her night table to wipe it off. Oddly, this small effort satisfied her.

Next she turned her attention to what was going on inside her head. Who should she start with? He had promised to call but he hadn't: she hated him for not living up to his promise. *Finito*! If he comes back, she will behave snobbishly and put a distance between them. She tried to imagine what this would actually mean. She would say hello and then go to another room, or maybe leave the house altogether. But no, this would not work: it is the reaction of one who cares. Maybe she should say 'hello', sit down and start talking as if nothing had happened.

She lit another cigarette and discovered while doing so that the distance between the opposite wall and the bed was disturbingly close: she felt the wall closing in on her and the picture hanging on it pressing against her breast.

A heavy hand knocked at the door, but she was busy focusing her hate on a friend who had left. 'I will not bring up my children in this country. It is a pile of garbage,' she had said. She felt like an empty can of sardines thrown into this garbage heap – the country? The heavy hand knocked again at the door, so she got up ready to hate whoever it was. It was the next-door neighbour asking to borrow some coffee.

Her hatred could no longer be contained. It showed in the smile she attempted to welcome her neighbour with and in the wooden box of coffee. The neighbour undoubtedly felt it, for she said nothing more and left abruptly.

While returning to her hideout she caught sight of her father glaring down at her from his portrait. 'It is difficult for me to be compassionate towards you today,' he said, and then added, 'may God have mercy on you.'

Translated by Ellen Khouri

Name-calling

'I got me the only rose on the family tree,' Mitch liked to say. When they were first married, Dolores took it as a compliment, and she'd colour a bit, looking rosier than ever. But after a while she caught on that Mitch was boasting about himself, not her. And, more than anything, was being mean about her sisters. 'The thorns,' he called them.

When the children came along, Mitch found a new twist on the joke. 'Get ready, kids. Uncle Al and Thorn Selma are coming over – whatever you do, don't let her hug you!' Or, with a shake of the head, 'Your Thorny Margaret, ain't she the sharp one!' Now that he'd got hold of it, he couldn't let it go. If one of his daughters answered back or made a face, he'd say: 'Uh oh, looks like we got a little sticker pushing out here! Where's my scissors?'

'Papa's just teasing,' Dolores told them, angry at him for getting them worked up, and angry at them for taking it to heart. 'Barbara the barbarian,' Mitch would mock the oldest, his way of making her obey. She blamed her mother. Other mothers thought about what they were doing, and named their girls something pretty, like Rita or Marilyn or Amy. Barbara took things into her own hands and called herself Babs. The younger girl was Theresa. 'St Theresa, cut that out!' Mitch would yell, though really she was the more obedient of the two. 'We could call you Terry,' was Babs's suggestion. But Theresa said no, that sounded like a boy's name.

Babs shrugged. 'Suit yourself, St Theresa.'

Dolores felt for her girls, but they'd get over it. It was she who made herself sad. 'You should take a baking class,' advised her sister Selma, drying dishes after Babs's sweet sixteen. 'Learn to frost a wedding cake, there's money there. Or get yourself a job. Look at me, you never see me bored.'

Dolores frowned. 'Did I say I'm bored?'

'I've got a place where they're expecting me five days a week, rain or shine, cramps or no cramps. If I miss, the operation falls apart.' Selma answered the phone at her husband's upholstery shop, and between calls reshelved the fabric books and vacuumed up the lint. 'Things are changing,' she explained. 'Ladies can have careers.'

Dolores couldn't think of a career and didn't want one, or any class either. She knew the name for what she wanted – flower power. She loved the sound of it. Once, at breakfast, she asked Mitch: 'What's this flower children business? Who gets to be one?' She was at his shoulder, pouring him his second cup of coffee.

Mitch twisted around to look up at her. 'You planning to apply? We got forms down the post office.'

'That's not what I mean,' Dolores said, turning her back to set the coffeepot on the stove.

'Better plan on dropping fifteen pounds. They got their standards, doll.' He was laughing hard now, letting it out almost choking on his toast and coffee.

'And don't call me doll,' she muttered inside her head. On their first date ever, he'd called her Dolly, short for Dolores. 'Please don't call me that,' she'd asked him nicely.

'Why?'

'I just don't care for it, that's all.'

He'd sighed. After that, he called her 'doll', which was worse, of course. But Dolores didn't have another protest in her, didn't want him to be mad. It was the same on their next date, when he unbuttoned her blouse and got his tongue in there. She kept her mouth shut, trying not to breathe in the pomade on his hair. Only gasped once when he pulled her on his lap and began bouncing her, slamming her into his crotch, fast and frantic, until, his fingers digging hard into her shoulders, he let out a howl. When he was through, Dolores didn't know what she was supposed to say or do.

Silly to bother about that now. She bought herself a spiral notebook with a paisley cover and started pasting in pictures from the papers and *Time* magazine. The first was one that Mitch himself had come up with. 'Here,' he said, shoving the magazine under her nose, making a point. 'See what the world's come to!' When he moved his thick forefinger off the page, she saw a girl, not much older than Babs, picnicking with her boyfriend. He was in shorts and bare to the waist. She was bare all the way but turned so you could just see the curve of her cheek, one breast and the roundness of her arse up close. She was pretty all over. Like a healthy toddler, Dolores thought. Like her girls when they were babies, running into her arms, their cloth nappies bagging down to their knees.

Mitch's thumb nailed the spot again, blotting out the girl's flesh. 'If I ever thought one of my girls ...!'

'They won't.'

'If you brought them up right.'

Later, with Mitch gone to work, Dolores scissored the picture out and scotch-taped it to the first page in her notebook. After that she kept the notebook hidden under the underwear in the top drawer of her dresser. She'd pull it out, when no one was around, to add a picture or turn the pages. For a long time, her favourite was a black-and-white shot of soldiers standing at attention while girls in thin summer dresses stuffed daisies in the muzzles of their rifles. Dolores didn't follow politics, but one thing was sure – those girls weren't 'fraidy cats.

But it was the soldier boys her eyes kept travelling back to, especially the smooth-cheeked youngster closest to the camera. There was something that touched her in the way he stood so still, letting the girl in front of him have her way. Probably he felt foolish, but he wasn't going to yell or make a scene. He had his orders, Dolores guessed. But what if the girl stuck her tongue out at him, what if she slapped his face, what if she kissed him on the mouth? 'He looks like a nice boy,' Dolores thought. Her mind went to her Uncle Sammy who'd married late and had a child when he was fifty. He'd let that little girl do anything she pleased. One day, when Dolores and her mother dropped in, Sammy answered the door with metal curlers in his wispy hair. 'We're playing beauty parlour,' he said and gave Dolores a big, fat wink.

Much later, when Dolores was grown up and a mother, she'd let her own girls brush her hair, curling it over their little fingers or bobby pinning it into a sloppy French twist. Sometimes they'd top off the 'do' with dandelions or stick buttercups behind her ears, then hold up a hand mirror so she could see. 'Look how beautiful!'

'Just call me Dorothy Lamour,' she'd agree, which made them giggle.

Underneath the photo with the soldiers the caption said

'flower power'. The first time she'd ever heard of such a thing. After that she saw it everywhere.

For instance, in one cartoon a crowd of college kids in beads and smocks and jeans, parading down the street, looking happy and as if they knew where they were going. But there was this cop in a phone booth. He was yelling, 'Chief! They're armed with petunias, marigolds and roses!'

Dolores kept staring at the kids in the cartoon, then in the mirror. Until one day she stopped curling her hair. Mitch knew something was different, but he couldn't put his finger on it. Of course, it didn't take Selma two minutes to spot the trouble.

'You're not letting yourself go to pot, I hope.'

'I'm not letting myself do anything.'

'You don't want to let yourself go.'

Every afternoon now, before the kids came home, she took her notebook to the kitchen table and set herself to studying the pictures, the same way she used to go at algebra problems, trying to crack the secret of x and y. Or the way she used to stare at models in *Seventeen* and *Mademoiselle*, to find out how to turn herself American-pretty. Her mother, who'd grown up in the old country, couldn't help her there, and thought it was all nonsense anyway. 'See how you worried for nothing,' she said, when Mitch from a good family back home popped the question.

After letting her hair go straight, the next thing Dolores did was to go into town and buy herself a pair of sandals. Not the pretty white ones with dainty crisscross straps and skinny heels – two pairs like that were already sitting in her wardrobe – but Jesus sandals, brown and flat, with sturdy soles that could stand up to rain and take a person any place they got a yen to go. Pretty soon, except for church on Sunday, she was wearing them all day and everywhere. Now she could take the dirt shortcut to the postbox without twisting a heel, could cut across the damp lawn and not leave divots, could stand at the kitchen sink and wiggle her toes.

At the kitchen table, with her notebook open in front of her, Dolores was working on a list: 'beads', 'fishnet stockings', 'tie-dyed shirt'. She'd have to go gradually, so that no one would notice. Like growing old, she thought. The folks who saw you every day didn't take it in, and then, before they knew it, you were dead. Except her plan was to go in the opposite direction.

She was drawing a question mark next to 'granny glasses' when Babs walked in on her. 'Ma, I've got to get my ears pierced.' Dolores flipped the notebook shut. 'I'm the only one left in the whole class. I need ten bucks right now, there's a nurse at Woolworth's.'

'You know what papa said.'

Babs waited.

'Okay, bring me my pocketbook.'

It wasn't 'til later, with the lamb and okra simmering for supper, that Dolores remembered what Babs had ahead of her. If she knew Mitch, he'd come to the table, take one gander – and bombs away! 'You couldn't wait to cross me, could you?' Babs would sit there in a pout, her hands in her lap, and, if she knew what was good for her, not saying anything.

But that's not how it played. By six o'clock, Babs was in a mood, every few minutes waltzing into the kitchen and hugging her mother. When Mitch walked in the door, she sashayed right up to him, couldn't wait to show off the evidence, tiny gold studs that had come home to roost. She lifted her curtain of hair with her arms, turned her head this way and that. 'Papa, don't I look pretty?'

'Isn't one hole in your head enough?' he grumbled. And let it drop. In bed that night Dolores dreamed of young soldiers in granny glasses nibbling her ears.

The next morning she phoned Woolworth's, and the person who answered said, 'Yup, 'til the end of the week.' She grabbed her handbag and headed out of the door. 'Might rain,' she thought; but she didn't turn back or wait for the bus.

Street after street, she was remembering things. When she was a girl, you wouldn't think to pierce your ears, not if you lived to be a hundred. Once, though, a new girl, as dark as Dolores and with little gold rings in her ears, came into the classroom. She could hardly speak English and her name was too long and too hard to say. Mrs Conlon led the little girl to the front of the room and turned her around to face the class. 'I don't think our new friend will mind if we just call her Frances.'

When Dolores reached Centre Street she slowed down, shifted her bag from one arm to the other and came to a stop in front of a bakery. She stared at the cupcakes and cream pies and then her reflection, trying to picture that little girl's face.

'What've you got on your ears, Frances?' At break, a fresh boy in the class came up close and pointed. Frances stood very still, her face red, her dark brown eyes ready to cry. 'What the heck are they?' He was showing off for the big kids. Two older girls shoved him out of the way, then reached over and twisted Francies's ear lobes 'til the tears leaked down her cheeks.

'Ugh!' one said. 'She's got nails in her ears!'

After that, only Mrs Conlon and the principal called her Frances. In the playground she had a naughty new name.

'Hey, Fannie,' children would yell, running circles around her. 'Hey, Fannie!' No matter which way she turned, they were tugging at their ear lobes and laughing their heads off.

At Woolworth's the woman behind the counter said: 'Make yourself comfortable, a couple of young girls are ahead of you.' Dolores sat on a stool by the jewellery case and leaned over to look at the studs. Tiny crosses, tiny pearl shapes, teensy daisies.

'The smaller the better,' she thought. The only jewellery her mother ever wore was her wedding band. But in the old country a gypsy woman had come around each spring, with needle and thread, to pierce the ears of the little ones. 'Did it hurt?' Dolores asked. Her mother couldn't remember.

Dolores had known other women from the village, some old enough to be her grandmothers. All dead now, her mother dead, too. When she was small, those old ladies gave her the creeps, and any time they dropped by to drink Turkish coffee with her mother or smoke a Philip Morris, she hid out in her room. But her mother always called her and made her kiss their damp cheeks and sit quiet while they gossiped in a mix of Arabic and English. 'Don't let them talk to me,' she'd pray. She couldn't bear to see the shiny vaccinations, big as silver dollars, on their arms; and their nylons rolled down to their ankles in summer; and the bedroom slippers they wore even to the supermarket; and especially their soft grey whiskers. Not to mention the holes in their ears. A long time ago, her mother's lobes had knit themselves closed. But these ladies must have been dumb as dishwater and put on heavy earrings every day. Dolores could tell because their ear lobes were droopy and yellowed, and showed gashes half an inch long. 'You could hang a camel from them,' her father used to say.

'You won't feel a thing,' the nurse said. She was standing at a little wooden table behind a curtain, and on the table was a towel and on the towel a metal contraption that reminded Dolores of pap smears. 'Don't worry about a thing, sweetie. I do this every day and nobody's sued me.' The nurse poured alcohol on a cotton ball and dabbed at Dolores's left earlobe.

'Tell me what you're going to do.'

'Well, I make a mark here, just where the hole should be. And then I staple the stud in.' She sounded matter-of-fact and cheerful.

'Make a mark?'

'Unless you'd like to do it, yourself, hon. Some people are very particular –they want it just so, not too high, not too low, not here, not there.

'Oh no, I trust you. Then what did you say is next?'

'The needle jabs right through here'– she kneaded one earlobe – 'the soft, fleshy part. That's the trick, you see? We don't want to run into cartilege.'

'It's not a big hole, is it?'

'Oh, no, dear.' She was brandishing the contraption. 'That's a good girl, try to relax.'

'Does it scar?'

'Shouldn't.'

'You mean it could?'

'You're a worrier, aren't you, hon? You know we could have been done by now.'

'I'm afraid I'm not very well,' said Dolores. 'If I'm better, I'll come back tomorrow.'

'Whatever you say. But we got this far, it's a shame not to finish.'

Riding home on the bus, Dolores was confused. Couldn't tell up from down, couldn't tell forwards from backwards. By the time she walked in the back door, she was feeling the way she used to after a killer maths test, sure she'd got an F and scared what her parents would say. Of course, this wasn't the same. If she didn't want her ears pierced, if she'd thought better of it, that was nobody's business.

She dropped her bag on the kitchen table, then went into the living room and curled up on the sofa. She'd forgotten about Mitch all day, but now she could hear him again in her head. From Day One of their marriage, he'd told her: 'You're my wife. Be normal, you hear me? Don't call attention.' And that's what she'd tried to do – what she'd always wanted even before Mitch came along. When she was a kid, she hated being almost dark as a coloured and having a mother who laughed too loud and sometimes spat right in the street, and old ladies around who didn't know the difference between slippers and shoes, and a father who reeked of cigars and tipped his hat to her girlfriends. Nobody else's father did that, not even to grownup ladies. 'Your father has a moustache,' the lady at the corner store said to her one day. And then the woman laughed, her thin lips thick with lipstick.

Now out of the blue, after all those years of not calling attention, she'd got this idea. Wanted something those girls in the pictures had, though she didn't know how to name it. But she'd only been fooling herself. Because how could she be like those girls who knew where they were going and weren't under anyone's thumb? They were so much younger and thinner and didn't have Mitch to answer to. Still, it was something deeper. No Old World in their head.

'It's all for the best,' she said finally, dragging herself up from the sofa and into the kitchen. Hungry for something sweet, she rummaged in the cupboard over the fridge. The bag she wanted was right where she'd stashed it, but ripped open and cleaned out, except for broken bits of chocolate and a heap of crumbs. 'Those were *my* cookies.' She shook the remains of the bag into her mouth. Her eye fell on a fresh jar of peanut butter, the girls' favourite brand that she'd bought them just yesterday. She unscrewed the lid and scooped out a fingerful, then stuck her finger in her mouth and sucked it clean. She experimented with forefinger, middle finger, ring finger, but her pinkie worked best. Scoop, suck, scoop, suck, 'til half the jar was gone and each breath she took tasted of peanuts.

Almost nauseous, she drew a glass of tap water to wash away

the taste. Outside, the rain had finally come, a vicious downpour. Through the window over the sink, Dolores could just make out the shuddering clothesline and, in the border along the fence, the bowed heads of dahlias, mums and late-summer roses. Could make out, too, where she'd gone wrong. Next time she'd print DOLORES in big, red letters on a sheet of paper and attach the paper to the bag with an elastic band. Or with a darning needle. Or with her mother's six-inch hat pin.

Mitch or the girls, it didn't matter. From now on, anyone poking where they didn't belong would be sorry.

Voice

She was standing in the kitchen when he came home.

'Who are you?' he asked, not yet concerned. Sometimes his wife hired a village girl to help the new maid with extra cleaning.

'Well?' he demanded, placing his briefcase on the table. 'What's your name?'

She merely looked at him with her frightened green eyes. They were huge in her pinched face. Her narrow shoulders slumped. She was so slight she might have been blown in through the doorway by a breeze. She had no hair to speak of, just a badly shaven mat, her scalp showing in some places.

'Don't you speak?' the man said. He was growing impatient. The maid's absence annoyed him. The vision of his return home had altered. He had wanted his Pepsi brought to him while he watched television, and he would put his feet on the ottoman and change the channels when he felt like it. He had installed a new satellite system that, as he liked to joke to his business friends, defeated all fronts in the war.

'Has my wife taken you on?'

After a moment, the girl shook her head.

'Where d'you come from?'

She looked bewildered. She had bruises on her arms and legs. Maybe she had been lost.

'You don't know where you come from?' he rephrased.

She shook her head.

'You don't speak?'

She did not respond.

The man had an idea. This would teach his wife for not adequately instructing the new maid. 'Do you cook and clean?'

She nodded uncertainly.

'Are you available to work?'

She made no sign that she was not.

'Then I'll take you on. Bring me a Pepsi when I've settled in the television room. They're in the refrigerator.'

He changed into loose trousers and a T-shirt and went to the television room. First, however, he stepped onto the veranda and examined his satellite dish, which towered over his opulent house and could be seen from any part of the village. It appeared flawless. It was perfectly round and shiny as when it had been installed two weeks before. Satisfied, he went inside. He settled on his easychair and placed his feet on the ottoman. He clicked the television on with the remote control and sighed. He had a good life. Despite these past difficult years of civil war, he had achieved a contentedness that few could boast. He had three handsome boys, a big house, cars, more money than he knew how to handle.

The girl came in with a Pepsi balanced on a tray.

'Ah, you're used to this,' he remarked happily, not thinking that most girls are taught to use trays, while boys are taught nothing about delivering food and drink to guests. 'My wife will be happy with you.'

The girl stood there. Her cheap trousers were torn and her short-sleeved blouse was grimy. She wore plastic sandals.

'My wife will give you clothing when she returns,' he said, feeling beneficent and enjoying his intrusion into household affairs, about which he knew nothing and which now seemed a mildly challenging game. 'And you can sleep in the shed outside. There's a pallet there. Let's see, what else?' he mused. 'Ah, you may eat meals in the kitchen. What, I don't know. And I'm sure you will have a day off now and then, but otherwise you should be here at all times.'

The girl remained where she was, hands behind her back and chin lowered. Her green eyes were fixed on the television screen.

'What else do you need?' he said, growing impatient. 'Is it your pay? My wife will decide that. I can't go that far!' he laughed.

Still she stood there.

'Go!' he barked, and she fled.

'What do you mean, you took her on?' his wife hissed. She was a slender woman who wore Armani outfits and heavy gold bracelets. She had been more beautiful when they married.

'I saw fit,' he said.

'You have no knowledge of these things!'

'She's our new maid!' he insisted. 'Don't argue with me!'

'We don't need one. And where's she from? What's her name?' his wife battered him with questions. 'Why does she have those marks on her? Who shaved her head? Why won't she speak?'

The man stamped his foot. She glared at him with her red lips clenched. He glared back.

'She'll probably never leave,' the wife said cautiously. 'Then she'll get pregnant with one of the village boys. Do you want a scandal on your hands?' she asked, gaining new momentum. 'What will people say about the little bald girl in our house, pregnant, unmarried? How will we get rid of her then? You want to cast out a pregnant girl?'

He stamped his foot and her mouth closed abruptly.

After a moment she said: 'But I'll have to dismiss the other maid.'

He glared at her so fiercely that she did not speak again, but left his television room, her high heels clacking on the marble floors.

The girl washed his feet with warm soapy water, softening the skin so she could pick out the corns that made him ache so. She had been with them a week.

'I like you, No-name,' he said. 'You do your work, you don't complain, you listen. My heart is heavy today. My children are unhappy. They're in school in Paris. Do you know where Paris is?'

The girl did not respond. Of course she did not know, the man thought, and this made him feel piteous.

'They are behaving badly in their school and the school wants to expel them. Expel them, I said? I was on the telephone with the headmaster, you see. Expel them? Don't you know there is a war on and they need to be away? How can you send them back into this danger?'

The girl patted one of his feet dry, then settled it on her lap and began picking at the corn with scissors. She frowned as she did this, as if concentrating very hard not to harm him, and he was moved. She looked better now, at least physically, and this was because of his thoughtfulness at taking her in.

'Look at you. You see? Had I not sent my children away they could very well have ended up where you are, depending on luck and the generosity of strangers. Few people are generous. You were fortunate when you walked into this house.' He smiled at her, but she was occupied with his corn and did not interrupt her work to show she had heard.

He fell silent for a while, his thoughts drifting during the not unpleasant sensation of having his feet handled by her small fingers. The new notion of his children having escaped the fate of the girl became more and more interesting to him. 'It is remarkable,' he said at last, 'how people can go from one place to another in their lives. The proverbial rich man suddenly loses all his fortunes and becomes a beggar on the street. Or the common whore gets lucky with a lottery ticket and becomes the toast of the town. Life,' he said philosophically, 'is unpredictable.'

The girl put his foot into his slipper and placed it on the floor. She gathered the napkin with the corn clippings by closing it one corner at a time and then deftly rolling it into a tight little ball. She threw the towel over her shoulder, picked up the scissors and the tub of soapy water, and left.

The girl's hair was slightly longer and the bald patches were gone, and they had discovered that its colour was a rich brown. Because her face was filling out and she now moved with more ease and grace, her appearance became important where it had gone unnoticed before.

'Are you Muslim or Christian?' the wife said. 'Maybe you are Druze.'

'She must be Christian,' the man countered. 'Look at those green eyes. No Muslim has such green eyes.'

'If you'd ever gone south, you would see that the Shi'a children have eyes like emeralds,' his wife said triumphantly.

She had only been to the south once, as part of a day trip to visit the United Nations posts, but the man was too tired to point this out. He worked hard all day.

'It doesn't matter what she is,' he said. 'She's still a fine maid. Better than the Sri Lankans.'

'If she's Muslim we could have problems.'

'How will anyone find out? She doesn't even speak to us.'

The wife admitted that the likelihood of the girl talking was slim, and so she gave up this concern. But she kept a secret eye on her. The girl had been so starved and shivering when she arrived that they had imagined her age to be younger than it was. She was prettier now, even though her expression hardly ever changed. Her bosom moved beneath her shirt when she walked, and her cheeks were plump.

The man looked for the maid because his siesta had been interrupted by the heat and he wanted the cool grenadine she made so well. She was not in the kitchen corner on her stool, nor could she be anywhere else in the house since those areas were forbidden to her except on cleaning day.

He stepped outside the kitchen onto the vine-shaded patio where they dined in the evening. Her shed stood behind this enclosure. He heard a sound and went to the shed and opened the door.

The girl was curled on her pallet with her knees to her chin, sobbing quietly. The man, disconcerted, put his head in to make sure he had seen correctly.

Her eyes met his and she leaped to her feet like a grasshopper. She wiped her nose.

'It's all right,' he said nicely. 'You can sit down.'

She hesitated, her fear evident.

'What's the matter?' he said. 'Sit down.'

She sat with her legs together and her hands on her knees. He settled beside her and smelled the olive oil soap on her skin.

'Why were you crying? Is it to do with whatever happened to you?'

Mucus was running from her nose and she ever so slowly raised her hand to wipe it away, as if trying to conceal this movement. Her fear induced in him a wave of need to give, and so he handed her his striped handkerchief.

'Go on, take it,' he said.

She took the handkerchief but did not use it.

'What happened to you that you came here and now you cry like this in your bed?' he asked. He wanted to know. The question had been bothering him since she arrived, but it was not until now that it surfaced so demandingly. Enough was enough. 'Answer.'

The girl stared straight ahead, and he saw that her shoulders trembled. He touched her shoulder and she made one jerking movement, much as a bird will dart inside one's hands before stilling itself, for every feather is in contact with the surface of its cage and it knows it cannot fly away.

'Why are you afraid of me?' the man asked irritably. 'I'm your helper. I've given you a house and food and easy work. You've got better under my care. Why won't you speak?'

The girl looked at him blankly. Her hands clenched each other in her lap, and the sight of this oddly reminded the man of the complex wires inside his satellite dish.

'Make me a grenadine,' he said, getting up. He wanted her to appreciate that he had stopped his questioning, but she did not appear grateful, and this annoyed him.

She followed him from the shed, her feet padding soundlessly in the dirt.

The guests laughed and drank and the girl hurried back and forth between the kitchen and the patio, bringing and taking as was demanded of her.

'She is a good maid,' the wife remarked. 'She never fusses, and of course is never on the telephone like those chatty Sri Lankans.'

'It's good to keep the economy inside the country,' one of the guests said, a businessman wearing relaxed tan slacks and Polo shirt. 'Those Indians send all their earnings home.'

'Where did she come from?' asked his wife, an Italian who had lived here for years. 'Perhaps her family is looking for her.'

'She won't speak.'

'Won't speak!' the Italian exclaimed. 'How unusual. Perhaps she is mute.'

'She has a tongue,' the businessman remarked.

'Well, now, how do you know that?' his wife said.

'I saw her lick her lips earlier.'

The two men laughed merrily and the Italian darted frowns at her husband. The evening was pleasantly warm and the scent of the grape vines above them permeated the air.

'No-name!' the man called. 'Come here for a moment.'

The girl came to the patio, her hands behind her back. Her hair, which was growing quickly, was proving to be curly and thick. She wore a white blouse and patterned skirt that had been handed down from an Ethiopian who worked for one of the wife's city friends.

'Our guests want to know why you won't speak!' the man said grandiosely. 'Perhaps now, at last, you will?'

He felt badly then, because the girl's eyes widened with fear and she shifted her feet miserably. Even his wife, who disliked the girl, gave him a reproachful look.

'You have no imagination,' she said to him. 'You,' she waved at the girl, 'go back inside.'

Afterwards they spoke of other things but periodically fell into uneasy silences, for the girl's mysterious story, clearly not a palatable one, had intruded on the dinner and poisoned their enjoyment.

The man came to the shed again and sat on the pallet with his legs crossed. He was wearing bright new tennis shoes and kept stroking the design on the side. The girl was sitting up smoking a cigarette rolled with paper. She smoked quickly and with great, deep breaths, filling the small area with pungent clouds.

'I keep thinking of your sadness,' the man said. 'I wanted to know what had happened to you, but since the other night when I challenged you before our guests I have changed my mind. There is something mystical about your silence.'

He gazed at the girl to communicate the depth of his change of heart. She smoked, obscuring her face behind the clouds. Her green eyes showed less fear, as if she felt protected behind this screen.

'It makes me feel poetic. Here you are, so silent. I wonder what your voice sounds like? What your accent is? And yet I don't need to hear it. I feel I know you without words. My wife uses too many words,' he chuckled, giving her a conspiratorial look. 'You know this, I'm sure. She uses words like the soldiers use bullets.'

The girl leaned over the side of the pallet, extending her long, slender arm to tamp out the cigarette in the dirt. The man kept his eyes on her movements until she was still again, her arms folded across her belly.

'May I touch you?' he asked politely, and he put his hand on her knee. It felt like a small, upside-down bowl. 'You don't need to speak,' he admitted. 'I like your silence. It surrounds me like fresh water.' He paused, impressed by his own fancy. He rarely felt such eloquent emotions.

The girl had begun to tremble and her lips disappeared into her mouth, whitening the skin around them.

'You must not be afraid,' he soothed. 'I'm a good man. You're like a daughter to me.'

He removed his hand, and the girl's face relaxed.

'You see?' he said, pleased.

But the man, later, could not take from his mind the feel of her knee inside his palm. He lay beside his wife at night, fretting.

He pictured the girl in the dark shed, curled beneath the blanket. He pictured her arm reaching out and down to extinguish the cigarette. He pictured her in the kitchen, moisture on her forehead and above her lip as she worked at the stove. Finally he slept.

'What is happening with the maid?' his wife demanded petulantly. 'Your eyes are on her all the time. You linger in the kitchen. You visit her shed. You drink too much Pepsi every day, and I think it is just so she can bring you another.'

'You're foolish,' he said, more irritated than ever by the accusations that had been raining on him for days. His wife would never grasp the treasure of his self-restraint. It had become his greatest joy to keep his hand only on the girl's knee and nowhere else, to prove to her that he could be trusted. One day she would speak to him. 'She is a helpless child. If you had had your way, she could be dead now, wasted.'

'And what a waste!' the wife snapped.

The man threw his hands up in despair. 'Haven't you finished?'

'Oh, you would like that!'

'Fire her if you wish,' he said impatiently. Perhaps the girl was not worth this daily sniping.

The wife was taken aback. She thought of the girl wandering off through the village and then onto the mountain roads. Soldiers lurked there. She could be shot, or worse.

'Go on, fire her,' he said. 'I want peace in my house.'

The wife snorted. 'You think I'm so callous?'

She returned to the kitchen and found the girl sitting on the stool in the corner, gazing out the window at the low, brown hills. Goat bells clanked dully from somewhere, and the air was dry and hot.

'What are you thinking?' she asked, though she knew it was futile.

The girl jumped off the stool, startled. She went to the stove and resumed stirring the beans.

The man placed his hand on her knee as had become customary. The girl no longer flinched, but kept a wary eye on him. He lit her cigarette and spoke.

'My boys are still causing trouble and the headmaster was insulted when I offered him more money to keep them. It seems at least one of them will have to return. I have arranged to have him picked up from the port since the airport is closed. Imagine, the headmaster sending a boy back to a country where even the airport doesn't function.'

He sighed. 'My wife thinks I'm interested in you,' he commented. 'She's frightened because you're so beautiful and silent, and she's aging and jabbers on against her will.'

The girl chewed the inside of her cheek, smoking.

'Is she kind to you?' he asked suddenly.

The girl nodded, and he was surprised.

'Truly?'

The girl nodded again.

'Please speak to me,' he said. 'I would like to know what happened to you, why you are here.'

She shifted her knee out from under his palm and drew her legs closer to her body so that her knees were beneath her chin. The material of her trousers tightened across her behind, which looked like the two rounds of a peach. After a moment, she lowered her legs and obliterated this vision.

'I care for you,' he said without thinking.

He was so upset by these words that he left abruptly, and the girl stared at the shed door swing until it stopped at half-open, leaving only a portion of the vine-covered fence visible.

The boy had grown taller and wore torn jeans and an untucked T-shirt. His hair was too long and his ear had a small, almost invisible hole in it.

'How could you do this?' the wife screamed, tugging at his ear. 'What are you? You know what people will think?'

The boy shrugged. His face was pale and sour.

The man commanded: 'Answer your mother.'

'Are you a homosexual?' the wife said shrilly. 'Is this why?'

The boy glowered at her and tried to leave the room.

'Stay!' the man barked, but the boy writhed out of his grip and stormed away.

'You see what Paris does!' the wife turned on her husband. 'He should have stayed here! Now he's become homosexual!'

'He's not!' the man thundered.

'He might be,' she hissed. 'How do you know?'

'If he'd stayed, he would've joined a militia and been killed. Is that what you want? You want your son to die rather than wear earrings?'

The wife sneered at him but did not answer.

'Leave him alone. He's a boy,' the man said, as if this explained everything.

The boy stayed in his room playing loud American music and smoking cigarettes. He sat hunched on the floor and scowled when his parents tried to come in. He did not go outside, nor did he eat with them. He made tapes from records and wrote in the names of songs in tidy, minuscule block letters. He lined up the tapes on his shelf and played them one by one. Sometimes he used headphones, and the house fell silent. The girl brought him Pepsi unbidden, and he drank it.

At dusk the man's hand settled on the girl's knee.

'You see how difficult my life is,' he complained. 'My son is a mutant and my wife despises me. Only my business is going well. And I thank God for these brief times with you, when I can unburden myself in your tender presence.'

The girl was eating a sandwich of honey wrapped in bread. Her sticky lips shone. She pushed her hair behind her ear and took another bite, then licked a finger.

'You like it?' he said, smiling.

She did not answer.

'What do you think about? Your family? Your village? You must be a village girl. Perhaps you were displaced in the war?'

The girl paused in her eating. Her large green eyes shone moistly.

'Tell me?' His hand tightened on her knee.

She did not.

He sighed, wondering at her resilience. 'I don't know why I ask, when I am fond of this silence,' he mused.

Dusk gave way to night and the cicadas began buzzing. The man sat with the back of his head leaning against the wall, eyes closed, her knee warm and moist beneath his palm. His fingers slid slowly a few inches up the soft fuzz of her thigh and stopped there. His stomach hurt with the strain of this delicate control. Her breaths became shorter, but when he opened his eyes he found her face taut with fear.

'I'm sorry,' he said brusquely. He got up to leave. 'I'm not perfect, you know.'

She did not move. Her teeth bit at her thumb.

'Don't do that,' he chastised, and left.

'Now we have two children who refuse to speak,' the wife muttered. She slammed pots and pans into the cupboard beneath the counter. The girl hovered about, unused to the wife's activity in the kitchen. 'Now I go from here to escape you, and I find him instead with his homosexual ear and torn clothes. I leave the house for a cocktail, thank God, and all I think about is him in his room, or you in your shed, and I don't know what you want or think or feel and it makes me so angry!' she shrieked, dashing a whiskey glass onto the floor.

Quiet fell. Rays of shards surrounded the opaque chunk that had formed the base of the glass.

'Sweep this!' the wife commanded.

The girl retrieved the soft, short-handled broom from the narrow cupboard and began sweeping, her bent form following the movement of her arm back and forth in waves. Her short, curly hair was pinned tightly back from her forehead. She had found a child's plastic pink barrette in the shape of a flower for this purpose.

'I'm sorry,' the wife said. 'I'm so tense, that's all. My husband is behaving strangely and my son is a monster. I hardly ever get to the city anymore because of the blocked roads and I miss my social times.'

The girl swept the glass into the metal dustpan.

'Uf, what a noise,' the wife commented, smiling, and the girl nodded in agreement, then went outside to empty the dustpan into the garbage.

The man found the boy on the patio with his Walkman, the tinny sound of music like a nail screeching on metal.

'Take that off,' he shouted.

The boy complied with a swift, irritated movement.

'What are you going to do with yourself now? You can't enter a school here. The closest one does not teach in French and you barely know Arabic anymore. I won't have you going into the city every day with all the danger.'

The boy shrugged and smiled with one corner of his mouth.

'You think this is funny?'

The shed door creaked open and the girl emerged. She walked past them with hurried bare feet, not looking at them. The man saw his son's eyes travel over her.

'But the danger is not so bad that we should not try. I

will call tomorrow.' The man sat back, satisfied by his son's disappointment.

At night the man went to the shed to speak with the girl but he heard a noise that gave him pause. He crept closer and pushed open the door to see his son moving on top of the girl, and then he heard her giggling softly. It shocked him to hear sound coming from her. Her slender arms were wrapped about the boy's shoulders and her curly hair was dark on the pillow. The boy grunted and the man stepped back, his body trembling with shame.

He stood in the darkness of the patio, listening. Time passed. Then the door opened and his son emerged into the moonlight, tiptoed past the vines and crossed the patio. The man remained in the shadows until the boy had gone inside.

He opened the door to the shed. The girl was already asleep, her naked body sprawled on top of the sheets. He saw the sheen of sweat on her skin. Her hipbones jutted above the dark spread between her legs. One arm was bent behind her head, the other hung off the edge of the pallet, fingers pointed to the floor.

He sat down and she woke. Her four limbs scrambled to cover herself, but his weight pinned the sheet and what was left of it reached only her belly. Her breasts were small but full, with dark, wide nipples.

He touched one and she made a whimper.

'You have disappointed me,' he said. His restrained, poignant adoration voided itself of meaning with the force of grain suddenly breaking through a flimsy sack and pouring out in a heap. The notion that she might have spoken to his son upset him further.

'Did you tell him?' he asked, his hand still on her breast, which shrank beneath his hand as she hollowed her chest, trying to ease away.

She shook her head.

He was bitterly pleased with her anguish.

'Tell me, now.'

She stared at him, uncertainty flitting across her features.

'Tell me or I will do what he was doing,' he said awkwardly, as if she would not know the name for it.

She lowered her head, obscuring her face.

He gripped her breast harder. 'Speak.'

A shuddering went through her body and then, to his amazement, she spoke. 'I was taken from my village when they attacked,' she said.

Her voice, so small and weak, shocked him. It did not approach any of the voices he had imagined for her. She had a faint lisp.

'Who attacked?'

She squirmed under his hand and he released her, for that had been his bargain. But his hand felt bare and cold now. She tugged uselessly at the sheet, which was still pinned beneath him.

'Go on.'

'The soldiers,' she said in her little voice. 'That's all I remember. Then I was here. I think a lot of time went by before I was here,' she added.

'Did they do to you what my son did?' he asked, for now this was the thing he wanted to know.

She did not answer. He heard her breathing, in and out.

'You can't remember?' he said.

She shook her head.

'Do you like it?' he asked. The question gnashed about inside his stomach. The wraith of his past obsession with her story flitted away.

She tried again to pull the sheet but he weighted himself down on it stubbornly. Her arms crossed her chest and she started to pull up her knees, but the sheet threatened to slide off completely and she lowered them again.

'I think you spoke to my son,' he said.

The girl shook her head.

'I took care of you,' he said. 'I was kind to you and told you my feelings and thoughts. I was patient with your silence, understanding. You repay me like this?' he tugged at the sheet but she gripped it against her belly with her elbows. 'You think you can play this game and get away with it?'

She shook her head fiercely.

'And then you finally tell me your story and it's so bare you might not have spoken at all,' he said. 'You were there, now you are here. What kind of thing is this to wait for as I did?'

The girl's lips shivered. She bit them. Moonlight filled the shed as the door creaked wider in the breeze.

'You will leave tomorrow,' he decided, and the pronouncement restored him. Sometimes kindness was ignored: this was the way of things, and he had to accept it as he did other facets of existence. He could not understand how for so many weeks he had endowed this creature with almost mystical properties, only to see her engaged in the most basic of acts, and to hear this bland little tale.

He wanted to stay. He wanted to remove the sheet from her trembling body and insert himself into her, biting her cheeks and nose and lips. He breathed deeply and rose. He patted her leg.

'You see how you were mistaken?' he said. 'You could have had a good life here.'

'How can you drive her off like this?' his wife shouted. 'She has nowhere to go and doesn't even know where she comes from. She's our responsibility!'

The man was astounded by her defence of the girl. 'I thought you despised her,' he spluttered.

'Perhaps, but I am not evil! She can't even recall her own name. She does good work here, and I'm used to her. And she talks now.'

'She has to go,' the man said, feeling the order of his house crumble about him. 'She is a whore.'

'No thanks to you,' his wife retorted.

'I never touched her!' he said at once, for this was paramount in his thoughts and he had been seeking the opportunity to admit it.

'You think I care?'

She was adjusting her gold earrings before the mirror. He noticed that her hair had been done at a salon and her nails were manicured. She wore a tight skirt and silk blouse, and her calf muscles were taut as she stood on her high heels. Suspicion touched him with its fiery little fingers.

'Where are you going?' he asked.

'To the city. I'm going to a party,' she said bluntly, and left the room.

Evenings, the man sat alone on the patio and smoked a waterpipe, listening to the distant rat-tat of gunfire, although sometimes the war paused and he heard only the cicadas in the trees. The girl's irritating laughter would float from the kitchen as she clattered dishes in the sink and regaled his wife with some village gossip. His son had left again, for America this time, a boarding school that accepted problem boys. The man's business was doing well despite the political situation, his wife had stopped the brief affair he knew she had had but which remained unmentioned between them, and his satellite turned this way and that, picking up the rest of the world. Occasionally, he invited some men from the village to sit in his television room, for he enjoyed their rapture at the large screen and at the array of broadcasts in foreign languages. At these times, they drank *arak*, served by the girl on a wide silver tray, the jug's mouth covered with an upside down glass and the rest of them in a circle around it. He still called her No-name, out of habit, though others had invented a name for her.

Her merry little voice in the kitchen irked him, so he was relieved when one day she married a boy from another village and disappeared from their lives. But he would go to her shed sometimes and lie on the pallet, remembering the story he had waited for and which had been so bland, and he wondered also how she must have felt beneath his son's gangly, teenage body. He was glad, however, that he had held his desire in check, for it proved that he was fundamentally a good man, and that it was not his fault that his kindness had been so disregarded.

HALA ALYAN

Painted Reflections

There is magic in these streets. Beirut, insolent as a rebellious teenager, pouty lips and all; shrewd as the middle-aged men who try to sell ribbons of air; as broken as the gun-riddled life occupying it.

This holiday has been years in the making, arising partly out of heritage (the gift my Lebanese mother left in my blood), and partly out of curiosity to see the growth of a city occupied with annihilating itself for so long. But still, the rusty research I did before coming did little to prepare me for the stark contrast between the steel and glass shrines in the renovated areas and the derelict buildings often right across the street.

I remember the way my mother used to speak of this country, eyes downcast, trembling voice, as though the words threatened to choke her. She would speak of a time before war as though in a distant dream, as though the country had never witnessed demolition and spilled blood. When I first saw the destroyed buildings, a shiver shot down my spine. Hatred had done this. A crack on the inside fuelled by those on the outside. The human instinct is to inherit rage and drown in vengeance. An eye for an eye, as the saying goes. Years ago, when I first came across an interpretation of that barbaric notion, I produced a painting. A disturbing piece entitled 'More Blindness'. Two androgynous young people with prominent, dark features stood apart, each holding a dripping, scratched eyeball and an empty eye socket. Their expressions were stricken.

There is a tiny part of me that wonders if coming here was the right thing to do. It's not so much the timing, but rather the country itself. I always intended to visit this place as a way of securing an invisible link to my mother's memory. Before her accident, we maintained a comfortable distance. She had never really forgiven me for the fall from grace that was my youth, and I didn't seek redemption. We fell into a pattern of bi-monthly phone calls and occasional lunches. But at least we talked. Father continues to ignore me and considers my older brother his 'only child'. He lives strictly by the glory of two things, the path of Christ and the stock market. Anything in between is secondary.

I tried writing when I was younger, but the words kept slipping away. I found myself chasing after vowels and dropping synonyms like uncomfortable clothes. But painting, expression through images and colours and brush strokes, formed something not only solid but also the opportunity to get a glimpse of myself on canvas. I feel like my soul is tucked away in the numerous tubes of paint that litter every place I inhabit.

I am severely tipsy by now. In the hotel room, the comforting warmth tingles through my body. I half-walk, half-stumble to the easel, the wine sloshing over slightly from the mouth of the glass. The blank canvas stares reproachfully at me, stemming a sense of urgency. This is it, the moment of adrenalin rush, when a million possibilities flash through my mind. Carefully, I set the glass down and locate a small knife on the table. My finger swiftly traces over the blade. The flesh rips obediently and I bring the finger to my tongue. The taste is metallic, thick and warm. Moving quickly, unable to see the marks in the dark, I smear my blood on the canvas, trying to project the image in my mind, alternating between my lifeline and the prepared palette. With no idea of what colours I am using or what shape is forming, I paint drunkenly, as if in a trance, enraptured by the slick sound of the moistened surface. My mind is saturated with images of run-down buildings, intricate jewellery, twinkling city lights. I feel my lips curl into a sardonic smile.

Something is wrong. Maybe it's the alcohol along with the tricks my substance-bruised mind sometimes plays on me. The painting seems ethereal, a rushed mistake of the gods. There is no beauty in it. Dark, clashing colours form an aura around the borders and there is an angry sky below. The blood I used flames scarlet in a thick haze. I am always surprised at the art I create in the dark, but it seems almost beyond me. I laugh sharply at myself. The feeling fades as I continue staring. It's beginning to look fine, despite all the crouching figures and, in the corner, an intricate upside-down cross. God is in the details. Or is it the devil? I suddenly feel weary. For some reason, Edgar Allan Poe's 'The Oval Portrait' flashes into my mind. It's the tale of a young woman, painted by her lover. He is transferring energy, lending her life to his canvas. Tiredness falls abruptly and, without bothering to change or switch off the light, I sink into a curled foetal position on the luxurious bed.

The next morning, I casually drop my head into my hands and massage my temples as I relax in the straight-backed chair at the Phoenicia café. Ah, hangovers!

To push out the pain in my throbbing skull, I begin to drift off into my thoughts, to recall episodes that haunt my mind.

I met Louis on a night after a rather questionable combination of dancing, drinking and acid. I stumbled onto him, in every sense of the word. We exchanged numbers and, eventually, worlds.

'So what are you going to do with it all?' He had asked me after an evening of conversation. An empty whiskey bottle was on the table, the glass catching the streetlights outside and splaying them on the wall.

'What do you mean?' I asked, blowing softly on my still-wet nail polish. 'Do with what?'

'With all this – your job, your life, your future. What do you want to do with it? Because if you don't want to spend the rest of your life slaving away in a nice little office from nine to six, now is the time to make a move.' He spoke casually, but there was something in the way his eyes caught mine. He cared so much that I couldn't risk losing him. His dark hair was rumpled, his shirt slightly open. Platonic friendships! Do they ever really exist? Yet with Louis it was more, so much more. This wasn't some drinking buddy or stand-in companion. He was going to be my saviour.

Everyone grows a little bit older, becomes slightly more bitter, but the bitterness is usually directed towards life, not faceless monsters. My loss was more personal than patriotic. No stars and stripes waved out of my apartment window. My tentative Arab heritage ended up being the source of a few catty remarks, but nothing more. We mourned our loss without succumbing to hatred, but it didn't make the absence any easier. Irony lives. I left New York, travelled around for a while, living off monetary proof that I, too, had once existed in a smart business suit, thinking I was getting away from everything, putting distance between myself and it all, only to discover that somehow I had unwittingly packed it all and brought it with me.

And what was 'it' exactly? I don't know. Perhaps it was the boredom, the restlessness, or the diminutive power of that city that I love as much as I hate the sudden fixation with painting. At the thought of painting, my fingers instinctively curve and I feel myself transported back to the here and now. I look down at them, at the various healing cuts on my fingertips, and my eyes turn away. I half raise my hand to ask for another glass of wine, just one more and then –

A crash sounds. No, not a crash, I realise after a bewildered second, louder, an immense barricade of reverberation so ear-splitting that for an instant I think I am deaf. For a split second, the thunderous roar leaves everyone immobile. I'm frozen with fear, instantly transported back to another time and place.

My God! What have I done, throwing myself into this battlefield? I'm dreaming, too much wine again. I'll wake up. But all those screams, it can't be a dream, and the sky seems as if it's falling. There's glass everywhere, I'm bleeding, Jesus, it's New York all over again, the panic, the fear, the smoke, only this is closer. Good God, am I going to die trapped in my own inability to move?

'*Yallah, Yallah*! Miss, you need to get out. Big bomb, yes? Come on, there's been an explosion. Please come.' Something in the urgency of his tone shakes me out of my stationary state and my legs begin to move, in a sudden homage to being alive, alive despite the stench of burned flesh that fills my nostrils as I stagger outside. The tumbling sunlight, slightly blotted out by thick black smoke, seems to taunt the terrified people who are fleeing the inferno, as if to say, 'Aha! You didn't expect this, did you?'

The smell, that awful reek of rotting life, enters me and clings to my very pores, my inner cilia. I begin to shake uncontrollably. The faces in front of me blur, the high-pitched shouts and cries become muted, and for a muddled moment I am six years old again, spinning too quickly, as the earth and sky become distorted, actually feeling the earth whirling on its tilted axis. My knees buckle and I crumple to the floor just as blackness swallows me.

Sunlight filters through my eyelashes as I am thrust back into consciousness. Almost instantaneously, everything comes flashing back – the explosion, the screaming people, the broken glass littering the streets and the revolting smoke. I bite down on my lip to keep from shrieking frantically, only to feel a stinging pain. I press down slightly harder and taste blood.

For one awful second, I cannot think. It's worse than when that thing went off, because then, at least, my mind was racing. But right now the only forming thought is the fact that I cannot keep grasp of a single coherent thought. Panic, bubbly in the back of my throat, begins to rise. In one second I'm going to lose control and join the wailing crowd with their hands outstretched towards the betraying sky.

For a bizarre second, I imagine my mother with them, begging the gods to take it back, to erase it all. Is this what she saw? The streaking smoke, the falling people? God's children falling like rain? And she was so young. All at once, I feel a rush of sympathy for the terrified little girl my tall, thin mother with her severe hairstyle had once been. This is not New York City, but Beirut all over again.

Instinctively, an instinct I lost when I was fourteen, my hand rises to my forehead and I begin to trace a cross. I despise hypocrisy and look at me now, turning to religion in a moment of need. I know, deep down, that the gesture is more one of childhood comfort than anything else, but I am still irritated at myself.

The panic has subsided now. Strangely, I feel detached, dream-like, as though nothing can penetrate my bizarre realm. There is a woman, looking frazzled, with an almost pained smile, speaking to some people at the hotel entrance. Feeling as though I am moving through the sticky, tangled strands of an enormous spider's web, I make my way over to her.

'Please, everybody, calm down. Please, quiet down.' It is as though this were all some twisted version of an unruly kindergarten class gone very, very wrong. I feel a pang of pity for this lady, probably just as terrified and clueless as everyone else, trying to be a pillar of unruffled calm. I imagine a massive canvas smeared with obscure blotches, and the Statue of Liberty rising from the centre, with tear-stained cheeks and thin lips. 'I will catch your tears in a bejewelled chalice. Here, let me bleed for you.'

The next few days are surreal. The country slides into a period of almost sinister mourning. I venture out into the city at night, when I feel too smothered by solitude, only to find barren streets and stores with obstinately locked doors. Everywhere I turn there loom enormous pictures of the former Prime Minister Hariri, looking purposefully into the distance. The city has turned eerie, its magic a warped and menacing Wonderland. I am taken to another hotel.

My strokes on the canvas are no longer caresses. They are desperate thrusts. I begin to close the heavy curtains carefully in the middle of day, forbidding slits of light to enter the room. In darkness, I paint outlines of the man they called Hariri, who I was told, had been assassinated minutes from his own handiwork; I paint flocks of weeping women clad in black; I paint bodies flying, limbs flailing, necks at an awful angle; I paint charred faces, eyes with pupils of smoke. I paint image after image of Louis, who has begun to creep back into my alcohol-induced days and nights, his eyes heavy with the promise of transience. I paint my mother, trying to stitch broken bodies back together with a terrifyingly large needle and thread, her fingers dripping with blood. I paint death, I paint grief. I paint loss and, what started as a depiction of the situation around me, turns into images of my grief and my loss. I have opened the stitches of a crevice for Louis to crawl through, and he does. My supply of canvas starts to run low and I begin to request paper, any heavy paper, from the receptionist downstairs. I avoid sobriety like the delusion I now know it to be.

I paint.

I paint.

My nightmares begin to litter the room. They feel like a sickness as they possess me. I am thrown back into my younger days of empty sex, of empty drugs, of cutting up line after line of cocaine, when a terrified part of my mind knows deep down that I'm not really doing the coke...it's doing me, and with an almost malignant pleasure.

The country begins to shake me awake. Almost unwillingly at first, I learn more and more about the politics. It is not a pleasant series of events, but then, few countries have been born or established without drenching their soil with blood. But the difference here is that history is happening now, there are no textbook lessons. And somewhere inside my veins courses blood that is linked to this place.

The entire country is bristling, a nation that is suddenly wide-awake and furious. The stunned, controlled respect and grief that laced the city immediately following Hariri's death seems to have exploded. I cannot demand entitlement to this pain. Scrawled writing appears on the sides of buildings, demanding (in no uncertain terms) that Syria get out. Groups of young men and women flock to the town centre near the grave of this political figure now transformed into a reluctant martyr; tents begin to pepper the area. At night, cars whiz by with flags flailing out, teenage boys stick their upper bodies perilously out of the vehicles as they yell random slogans in Arabic. Demonstrations and counter-demonstrations begin. Voices demand freedom and truth. I go to these demonstrations as an onlooker only: I cannot demand entitlement to this pain. Yet I understand it. I've seen it before. I have come here to be distracted and this country is as distracting as I could hope for.

Several days after the counter-demonstration I sit in the hotel lounge, sipping black coffee and inhaling my cigarette. Ciara, a photographer I met before the assassination, walks over.

'Hey,' she says, 'Do you mind if I join you?'

'Of course not. How are the pictures going?' I know that, like me, she had made the decision to stay longer. For her photography, she said. I hadn't asked if that was the only reason.

'Actually, I was hoping to run into you. Would you like to see my work?'

'Sure.'

The first photograph shows a crowd of people at the demonstration. The second picture captures an old lady silently grieving. In the next photo a young man, in a sea of demonstrators, is holding up a crucifix in one hand and a Quran in the other.

I don't speak. I continue staring at the black-and-white depictions of life in front of me. I wonder what it must be like to see the world from behind a camera lens, to have that distance from everything awful and painful, yet still maintain the ability to capture it.

The last time I saw Louis, he gave me a sliver of hope.

The next day, a plane flew into a building. For the rest of the world, it was a 9/11 crisis, national tragedy. For me, Louis decided against a lunch break and was swallowed in the flames.

The demonstrations continue but my own thoughts are finally losing the edgy chaos. I wish I knew how I found this calm. It keeps me awake at night as I wonder, with unbelieving gratitude, what brought it on. My dreams are still vividly coated with images of my mother, of Louis, of the personifications of my mistakes, my losses. I wake up with my cheeks stiff with dried tears, but the smile I offer my mirrored reflection has lost its sarcastic resentment.

I decide it is time to leave.

The plane lazily lifts its nose and saunters to the skies. I swallow tears. I have got what I need. I can face what awaits me now. Below, the nightline of glimmering lights gently embraces the landscape and, like some intoxicatingly beautiful but dangerously poisonous flower, Lebanon winks at me and whispers goodbye.

The One-eyed Man

We shuffle forward, a jagged line of sorts. There are at least fifteen people in front of me, yammering, jabbering and exchanging their own foreign-accented versions of what happened in tongues made loose by tragedy. Even when I cannot understand what they are saying, I can tell from the gestures, the wide shining eyes. The bits and pieces they each saw are embellished and put together like so many pieces of a puzzle, given form in word and sign. These are the bonds of shared calamity. I remember them from nights spent in the crowded shelter while the bombs shrieked their banshee curses overhead. Neighbours were made lifelong blood brothers for that one night, for that one week, for however long it took us to trust the silence and creep back upstairs, back into the shells of our lives.

It would be so easy now to walk away. To slip out of the line and make my way to the waiting lounge. It's only a couple of hours until my plane takes off, and I have a magazine in my messenger bag. I am always prepared for the maddening tedium of transit: I have crossed these oceans before. But the line moves again and I move with it.

'Oh yes, in the bathroom they found him, my friend saw him. He was laid out right there on the tiles, as dead as can be.'

The sizzles of the Spanish accent come from behind me. I could turn around and tell them what I saw, proffer my own piece and use it to link myself to them. But I learned from my father that no words carry the weight of a heart made heavy by solitude. He told me this with every hour he spent smoking his pipe in silence, sitting in his chair in the corner of the living room of our house in Beirut, mourning my mother's passing.

They buried him yesterday in his white shroud. It is Muslim ordinance, to feed the body back into the earth before it begins to decompose, before it starts bearing more resemblance to death than to sleep.

It is dawn in Toronto when the phone rings. Kathryn stirs beside me but does not wake: her sleep has always stretched into the luxurious depths of those who have lost the animal instinct to be ready to wake and run. I pluck the phone from its cradle to hear Lulwa, the youngest of my three sisters, on the other end of the line, her frayed voice reaching across the miles and years that lie between Beirut and me. She was the one who found him, glassy-eyed in his old chair, caught in a ray of afternoon sun, the dust motes dancing around his head. 'It's been eight years, Ali,' she sobs. 'We need you here. You can't not come home for the funeral.'

The unspoken implication slips itself like a noose over my head and pulls me, through the phone call to my boss – 'My condolences A'war. The other four programmers can pick up the slack, no problem. See you in a week,' – past Kathryn as she walks out of the door – 'It's over Ali. I can't do this with you anymore. My things will be gone from the apartment by the time you get back,' – onto the flight that deposits me here, at Heathrow, where

I await the final leg of the journey that will carry me home after eight years.

I am now the man of the family. This is what Lulwa says, and does not say. It is the fate promised me ever since my parents saw the longed-for penis between my legs – 'After three daughters, *al-hamdullah*!' and my father confidently added the 'And Son' after the 'Al-Awar' on the sign above his shop door. Although I am the youngest, although Ibtisam, Mimi and Lulwa are all grown up and married now, with children of their own, the duty falls on me to set my father's affairs in order and to minister to the mourners who have already begun to gather at his house.

I call home when it is clear the flights will have to wait out the heavy storm. I shovel the strangely thick English coins into the slot and dial the number I've never forgotten, not once in eight years. Ibtisam, my eldest sister, answers.

'*Allo*?' I know the clipped tones of her voice so well, even though it's become gravelly with cigarettes over the years.

'Ibtisam. It's me. Ali.'

'Ali.' With one word, her voice breaks then finds its hard shell again. In the background I can hear the desolate rise and fall of the sheikh's voice, singing the Koranic verses of mourning.

'What time are you arriving?' All business. I never remember Ibtisam wasting tears over anything, not like Mimi, and not like Lulwa, who cries so easily.

'There's been a delay, a storm. They've grounded all the flights out of here. I have to wait. I don't know how long.'

'Damn, Ali!' And she does cry, strangled, rasping sniffles that reveal her tension without dissipating any of it.

'I'm sorry,' I say, except I'm not, not really. I want to postpone arriving in Beirut as much as possible. I want to postpone greeting my sisters, seeing what eight years of the city and marriage and motherhood have done to them. I want to postpone arriving at my father's house, bereft of my father and greeting the mourners who will look at me accusingly, who will ask me why I've never visited before.

'I'll call you when I know more, OK? Give my love to Mimi and Lulwa. Tell them I'll be there soon.'

'Ali!' But she is cut off by a cool female voice, telling me to insert more coins if I want to talk longer. I don't. I drop the receiver back into its cradle, aware of the long line of people behind me, impatient, waiting.

The line moves again. I stay. What is it Alexandra said at dinner? 'No one can change the past. But that doesn't mean the future isn't still salvageable.' I want to believe this. I want to share her optimism. She is lobbying for a plot of land in central Beirut; she wants to rescue it from the developers, who are only too eager to buy up every last inch of the city's shattered heart and make it bleed money from its bullet holes. She wants to create a garden out of the ruins. A garden of forgiveness, she calls it.

'What makes you foreigners think you can just come to our country and fix us? You think we did not know civilisation before you? Bibles, guns, flowers, it's all the same!'

And this is what I never told Kathryn, why I never told Kathryn anything but the barest essentials.

'Tell me about Lebanon,' she would say, propping her head on her hand, or curling into my lap. 'Why did you leave?'

'Because it is the shittiest place on earth. It's a garbage dump. You don't believe me? There's a mountain of garbage stretching out into the sea.'

'*Ali*! You can't just turn everything into a joke you know.' Then, with her husky voice and wide blue eyes made soft by the very idea: 'Was it the war? Is that why you hate it so much?'

No, I wanted to say, it was the peace I hated more, but I didn't know how to tell her this. She, with her Canadian life, with her endless northern summer days spent loping across green lawns, biking through residential streets wider than a Lebanese highway. She, who once volunteered at the soup kitchen, and spent the evening crying. She, who thrilled to the touch of the crescent-shaped knife scar on my shoulder. There are times when hearing her chatter away about something she has read about my country makes me want to shake her until her teeth rattle, until I wipe the fascinated look from her face and see it contort instead into uncertainty and fear.

That rage I kept hidden from Kathryn I unleash upon Alexandra, whom I have just met at dinner, who does not know I have just looked into the glassy eyes of a dead man after I thought I was done with all that.

'I lived through the war too, you know. I married into it you could say.' She speaks calmly, quietly, and I expel the breath I have gathered in preparation of another blast. She looks and sounds so English. And yet her last name, when she tells it to me, begins with the same guttural sound as my own, unpronounceable to those whose throats aren't long used to the necessary excavation.

'A-*war*,' Kathryn says when I first tell her my name. 'And you're Lebanese. How appropriate.'

'No,' I tell her. 'A'war. It means one-eyed. The king in the kingdom of the blind.' This makes her giggle.

She is the one who asks me out, undeterred by my mumbling, my awkwardness. She is beautiful, and that is part of the reason for my hesitation. She is also frightening. Her blonde hair and white teeth, the way she speaks, so enunciated, her snub nose and blue eyes: everything about her is sharp and percussive in its impact. I am afraid she will cut me. Even when I get to know her, when I understand that the precision of her features bespeaks the quality of her mind and not of her nature, I am still wary.

She wears me down, in her own laughing way. 'What a

strange accent,' she says when we first meet. And, later, during one of those first few enchanted dates, she raises her eyes to mine and proclaims it 'incredibly sexy'. And so I learn to ask for things – the bill, directions, more wine – without the shameful apology of the immigrant when she is by my side. Everything I find most loathsome about myself she is infinitely fascinated by.

I tell her a few things. How I lost my mother to cancer in '83, when I was nine. How during the endless summer of '82 while the Israeli tanks rumbled in from the south and pierced into the alleyways of the city, she lay dying, her blood slowly turning to poison in her veins. I do not tell her about keeping vigil in her dark room, watching her skeletal frame lit up by the shells that exploded like fireworks in the summer night and thinking that even then, at the very end, there were still many ways for her to die.

I tell her how my father has not spoken to me since my immigration to Canada was approved. How he bequeathed his shoe store to Ibtisam's husband, the shoe store that made its own killing during the war, for the worse the fighting got, the more Lebanese women seemed to have a taste for Italian leather shoes.

Kathryn loves this last piece of information. She sees in it only a fierce will to live and not the absurdity of material vengeance. She has never seen these dainty shoes step lightly past armless, legless beggars in the streets.

Every year we are together she asks: 'When will I get to visit Lebanon? When will I meet your family?'

At first the dark look in my eyes holds sway, swallowing the questions. Then at some point the fighting begins. She is a better fighter than me. It's the fluid English she speaks, all slurred gerunds and flat vowels. No rolling of the 'r's for her, no mixing up of the prepositions. No loss of momentum or sudden spluttering and dying out when you're halfway to making your point.

There are only nine people ahead of me now. I bolt out of the line, and my place is swallowed immediately. Then I remember that I will meet Lauren again in the waiting lounge. We are on the same plane bound for Beirut. I stop. The thick coins jingle in my pocket. They are all I have left of England and I wish to be rid of them before I go. 'I'm sorry,' I say to the Spanish woman who was behind me. 'I thought I heard my flight being called.' She scowls but moves back and I squeeze into place once more.

'People can't help who they are,' Alexandra tells me. 'You can't hate people because they want to help, or because they don't know how.'

'Help!' I say, tearing savagely at a piece of steak. 'As if we are dogs who need taming!'

'You're right,' she says, after I have chewed and swallowed. 'But not all help is patronising. There is no one who doesn't need help. You just have to listen to what drives it, I think, love or pity.'

My father does not ask for help in those days after she leaves us motherless. He leaves me to my sisters, leaves us all to each other, and shuts himself up in his shop. At night he smokes and smokes. He speaks mostly to Ibtisam, who is eighteen. He asks her what we need by way of clothes, money and food. We want for nothing, except for what he cannot give us.

When Kathryn wakes, I tell her what Lulwa has told me. She cries, at first for my father, and then because she understands I will not let her come. I tell her there is no reason for her to come, that she will complicate things for me. She rails and thunders, says that I shut her out, that I do not allow her to share my grief, that I am ashamed of her. I yell back. I swear at her in Arabic, a filthy string of gutter talk she would shudder at if she understood. She recognises the implications of the words, but stands her ground.

'Stop it,' she sobs. 'I want to be there for you. I want to help you through this.'

'Go find yourself another immigrant charity case to cry over!'

And this is when she breaks down, when her sharp features come into focus under the blur of tears, when she says, 'It's over Ali. I can't do this with you anymore. My things will be gone from the apartment by the time you get back.'

The line moves forward, too slowly.

Behind me the Spanish woman and her companion are still talking.

'There was an inquiry. They caught the people responsible.'

'I can't believe there was a terrorist loose in the airport.'

'I know. But they've interrogated all the questionable people. They said everyone was cleared.'

'Still, I won't feel safe until I'm back in my house with my husband and children.'

They take us to a small, blank room, flanked with benches. There are other people there, all men, mostly my age. They all have the same dark, angry eyes.

'There are some things that cannot be forgiven,' I tell Alexandra.

One of the older bearded men in the room roars at the airport authorities.

'Why are you keeping us here? What is the meaning of this?' His voice rises angrily. 'I am a professional! I run a business in Peshawar! I employ people like you!' He points accusingly at a uniformed man with tamarind-coloured skin identical to his own.

'He is so strong,' say the friends and neighbours who see my father hard at work in the months after the funeral. 'The children are lucky to have such a committed father.'

He never tries calling me, not once in eight years. I do not call him, either.

I take one more step forward.

His glazed eyes look straight into mine, and for just a second, I want to help him. Then I understand that he is beyond any sort of help I can give him.

I tell the airport authorities what I saw. I tell them I saw a dead man in the bathroom, sitting dumbly on a toilet bowl, his face an ashen purple above his necktie as if it marked a boundary where anonymity begins. I do not tell them about his shirt, grey from frequent washing, threadbare and shiny under the fluorescent lights. I do not tell them of the look on his face, a look of supplication, of horror, of sheer dumb surprise, a look that says: 'I didn't think I would go like this. I didn't think my death would be so meaningless.'

I am led by two men, one dark, one blond, into a small room, bare but for a small window, three chairs and a metal desk that takes up half the space. Two of the chairs are placed behind the desk, one opposite it. It is clear that this is the chair meant for me. My stomach contracts, my jaw is set. I am prepared for this to turn ugly, to have to deny past plots and present involvements. The blond man seats himself behind the desk and starts riffling through papers, amongst them my passport and ticket. The tamarind-skinned man stands behind him solemnly, overseeing this ritual. His nametag reads PJ.

'Neither business nor pleasure,' I answer. 'I am going to Beirut to attend my father's funeral,' and when I say this, I finally understand what it means.

I look into his dead eyes and think, how wretched. How final. How unforgiving.

'Forgiveness is the only recourse we really have,' says Alexandra.

'Otherwise, what is there for us really? You know that the war is still a taboo subject in Lebanon because we can't talk about what happened without implicating everyone in the crimes that were committed. But at what point does the blood feud end? How can it end if we never talk about it?'

The city is a landscape of scars and bruises. I cross the green line alone for the first time, unchecked, looking out for sniper fire but hearing only the silence of car engines thrumming in the traffic. I discover a new half of my city, my country. Here there are nightclubs by the sea and tired Eastern European women swaying their hips in umber bars. The boredom settles in and it is stifling, like heat. Everywhere there is construction, new façades put up to cover the past. The older people do not talk about the war. It is only we who repeat the litany of close calls, of near brushes with death, and even when we have learned them by rote, we do not tire of hearing them. It is our secret that we feel cheated out of this war, that we never strutted the streets with our Kalashnikovs held at proud attention. That our only experience was to lie like cowering dogs, robbed of our childhoods by the acrid taste of fear and sweat.

'I have done nothing wrong,' I say.

I look at PJ silently placing myself in his hands. He will be the one who understands. PJ scowls and leans across the desk.

'You'll wait until we're finished going over your papers, yeah?'

At university I decide to study computer engineering. Machines reveal their inner workings far more easily than people. It is the way of the future, and the future is far from Beirut.

'Your life is here!' My father roars. 'What have I been working for all these years if not for you, if not to give you a better life than the one I had?'

'We have to start dealing with each other as human beings,'

says Alexandra. 'In that sense the war was like a long period of amnesia. We forgot how to deal with each other. Only you can reclaim your own humanity – no one bestows it on you. It is not a favour, it is a right.'

There is one last woman ahead of me, an Indian woman in a colourful sari. She is excited because she is finally going home.

They let all of us go after the investigator ascertains that the man in the bathroom died of natural causes. We are escorted to the Heathrow Hilton and given time to wash up and rest before dinner. It is their way of apologising for the delay, for the inconvenience of the inquiry. There is a lot of meat on the table. The Lebanese do the same when they wish to put their best face forward.

Until the smell assails my nostrils I think I will be unable to eat meat. Then I eat like a castaway, ravenous, savage.

A middle-aged woman with mirthful blue eyes sits across from me. I try to ignore her, as I have ignored everyone so far, until I am forced to ask for the salt. She passes it to me and smiles. 'Hello. I'm Alexandra. Where are you headed?' I hesitate.

It is Christmas. There is an office party for the staff at the elementary school where Kathryn works. She has somehow convinced me to come. I am wearing a red sweater she has knitted for me, a gift. She tells me she doesn't like to just buy things for people she loves. And this is how I discover that she is in love with me.

I am drunk on wine, on being here with her. She stands across the room under the mistletoe. She explains what this means with the crook of her finger, the pucker of her lips. I am about to go to her when I am accosted by one of her colleagues, his wine-soaked smile gracing a face the same shade of red as his hair.

'Omar, was it?' he asks.

'No, Ali.' I am polite, but already wary.

'Whatever. Listen, Kathy is a good friend of mine, a real sweet girl. I better not hear of you roughing her up or disrespecting her. I know how you people treat your women.'

I say nothing. Kathryn beams at me but I cannot look her in the eye. I spend the rest of the evening avoiding all her colleagues, evading further introductions. Later, in the car, she tells me she heard from her boss that Pete was rude to me, that he was drunk, that he is usually a fine man. I say nothing, and I roll away from her in bed when she tries to reach for me. She does not understand.

Is it love or pity?

She practises pronouncing my name. 'Ulli,' she says, not 'Alley,' as most everyone else does, and I smile. One night she makes me *tabbouleh* from a recipe she gets off the Internet. I eat it and say nothing, chewing the unsoaked bulgur with difficulty. She has merely garnished it with parsley and forgotten to add lemon juice and pepper.

She leaves small gifts around the apartment, articles I might be interested in like books and brochures for trips we can take together. She shows me the Rockies like a revelation she has prepared especially for me on a train ride through the Prairie Provinces. She takes me to meet her parents in British Columbia. The house is noisy with grandchildren, warm with cooking and easy laughter. Her father takes me salmon fishing. Across the river we see a bear lumber through the bushes, a mass of muscle rippling smooth under sun and water-dappled fur. I am so dumbstruck by the sight that I forget to be afraid.

'Tell me about Lebanon,' she says, curling into my lap. 'There is nothing to tell,' I say.

'I want to help you through this.' Her face is precise and birdlike behind her tears.

'Oi! Mate!' yells a man somewhere down the line. 'There's a

bloody 'orde of us waitin'! Get on wiv it!'

I pick up the receiver. It smells of garlic and sandalwood. Like Ibtisam's cooking, like Kathryn's incense.

I dial the number. It rings twice.

'Hello?'

'Kathryn?' I can't help it. I start to cry.

Biographical Notes

ETEL ADNAN is a widely acclaimed Arab-American poet, writer, essayist and painter who was born and brought up in Beirut. From 1958 to 1972 she was Professor of Philosophy in California. Adnan is the award-winning author of *Sitt Marie-Rose* and *The Arab Apocalypse*. Many of her poems have been set to music by contemporary musicians, namely Gavin Bryars, Tania Leon, Annea Lockwood, Henry Treadgill and Zad Multaka. She collaborated with Robert Wislon on his opera *Civil Wars* and her two plays, *Like a Christmas Tree* and *The Actress* have been performed in San Francisco, Paris, Dusseldorff and Bad Hamburg. Adnan's most recent work, *In the Heart of the Heart of Another Country* is published by City Lights and 'The Power of Death', initially appeared in *First Intensity* (2002).

RIMA ALAMUDDIN was born in Beirut to a Druze father and a Swiss Protestant mother. After receiving a BA from the American University of Beirut, she continued her studies at Girton College, Cambridge. Alamuddin wrote her first novel, *Spring to Summer*, at the age of nineteen followed by a short story collection. *The Sun is Silent* was published in 1964, a year after her tragic murder by an unrequited suitor.

HALA ALYAN is a sophomore student at the American University of Beirut who has lived in New York and the Middle East. Alyan considers writing a vital part of her life.

JOCELYNE AWAD is currently editor-in-chief of *Mondanité* magazine. Her novel, *Khamsin* (2004), received the France Liban and Richelieu Senghor prizes and her latest work, *Carrefour des Prophètes* (1994), has recently been translated into Polish.

LAYLA BAALBAKI, born in 1936 to a conservative Shiite Muslim family in south Lebanon, made an instant name for herself with the publication of her first novel *Ana Ahya* (*I Survive*, 1958), which was translated into French and other European languages. Two years later her second novel, *al-Aliha al-Mamsukha* (*The Disfigured Gods,* 1960) was published, followed by *Safinat Hanan ila al-Qamar* (*Spaceship of Tenderness to the Moon, 1964),* a collection of twelve short stories.

HODA BARAKAT, an award-winning novelist, was born in 1952 and worked as a teacher, translator and journalist in Lebanon before moving to Paris to become a full-time writer. Her debut novel *Hajar al-Dahik* (*The Stone of Laughter*, 1990) won the al-Naqid Literary Prize for first novels. It was followed by *Ahl al-Hawa* (1993), *The Disciples of Passion* (2004), and a collection of essays, *Rasa 'il al-Ghariba* (*The Letters of the Stranger*) published by an-Nahar in 2004.

NAJWA BARAKAT was born in 1960 and moved to Paris in 1985. She has worked as a journalist for a number of leading newspapers, including *al- Hayat* and *an- Nahar*, as well as a scriptwriter, radio commentator and translator. Her book *Bas al-Awadim* (*The Bus of Honest People*) was published by Dar al-Adab in 1996 and won a major literary prize in France. *Ya Salam* was published in 1999 and *Lughat as-Sir* (*The Language of the Secret*) in 2004.

SLEIMAN EL-HAJJ earned a BA in English Literature and a BS in Biology from the American University of Beirut. He was chief editor of the university science newsletter, *Bits and Pieces of Science* (2003–4), and has worked as a freelance journalist for the past two years. Currently El-Hajj is a graduate student at AUB.

JANA FAOUR ELKADRI was born in 1980 and graduated from the American University of Beirut in 2001 with a degree in Business Administration. She has worked as a freelance writer for the *Nahar al-Shabab* supplement and currently she is in the advisory division of Price Waterhouse Coopers. Elkadri lives with her husband, Abdul Aziz, in Toronto.

ZALFA FEGHALI is a Lebanese-Cypriot who was born in 1983. She holds a BA in Political Studies and is currently working on an MA in English Literature at the American University of Beirut. Feghali wrote 'Wild Child' for a Creative Writing workshop.

ZEINA B GHANDOUR was born in Beirut and grew up in London. Her first novel, *The Honey* (1999), was published by Quartet Books and translated into a number of languages. Ghandour's essays and short stories include *The King of Lospalos and I: A Guide to Rum Sours: Observing Elections in Haiti*; and *War Milk*. She has worked for various human rights agencies and international organisations in the fields of legal research and election monitoring. Ghandour is currently completing a PhD at the London School of Economics.

MAI GHOUSSOUB is an artist, author and publisher. Born in Lebanon, she moved to London in 1979 where she co-founded Saqi Books. Her work includes *Leaving Beirut*; *Women and the Wars Within*; *Postmodernism*; *The Arab in a Video Clip*; and *Male Identity and Culture in the Modern Middle-East*. Ghoussoub's artistic output has focused on installations that explore themes of immigration, shifting identities and transexuality. She has written and directed *Divas, for Jamil/Jamila* a performance play shown in Beirut, London, Paris and Newcastle. Her latest performance/play, *Texterminators*, was shown at the Lyric Theatre, Hammersmith, the Dominion, Southall, and most recently, at the Marignan Theatre in Beirut.

MERRIAM HAFFAR left Lebanon with her family during the war years to live in the US and the United Arab Emirates. In 2005 she graduated from the American University of Beirut with a degree in Biology and is currently pursuing a graduate degree in Environmental Sciences and Management at Ryerson University, Toronto. Haffar enjoys writing during her spare time.

RENÉE HAYEK was born in 1959. She received her BA in Philosophy from the Faculty of Letters at the Lebanese University and worked as a journalist before becoming a teacher at the Collège Protestant in 1980. Her postwar short story collection, *Portraits of Forgetfulness* (1994), won the first literary prize at the annual book fair held in Beirut that same year.

MIRNA HAYKAL received her BA in English Literature from the American University of Beirut. She is currently completing an MA in Medieval Literature and hopes to pursue a PhD in the near future.

HOUDA KARIM studied French Literature at the Lebanese University and later taught in a number of public schools. During the war she left Lebanon with her family and while residing in Paris she produced her first novel, *Lézardes* (1999). Upon returning to Beirut she wrote *Houriya* (2004), and her latest novel, *A Slice of Beach* (*Tranche de Plage*) is forthcoming. Karim's novels are set in Lebanon and inspired by the lives of young students she came to know while teaching in Beirut and South Lebanon.

ELLEN KETTANEH KHOURI attended the University of London's School of Oriental and African Studies, where she specialized in Middle East Area Studies and obtained an MA in Political Science. She started her career as a Jordanian diplomat, serving in Bern and Switzerland before establishing the Al Kutba Institute for Human Development, a human rights and democracy organisation in Amman, Jordan. Khouri has worked as a consultant on human rights and democratisation with the European Union Commission Delegation to Jordan and participated in a European Union-sponsored training course on election monitoring. She lives and works in Beirut as a freelance human rights and democracy trainer, and translator.

MAY MENASSA, a journalist since 1968, writes regularly for the cultural section of *an-Nahar*. She is the author of three novels: *The Pomegranate Notebook* (1998); *Pages of a Prisoner's Notebook* (2000); and *The Last Act* (2002). Her most recent publication is a children's book entitled *Dans le jardin de Sarah* (*In Sarah's Garden*) (2005).

LINA MOUNZER was born in Beirut in 1978 and moved to Canada with her family just before the Lebanese war ended. She returned twice on her own, the second time dropping out of university to pursue various career options including teaching and editing. In 2004 Mounzer graduated with a BA in English Literature from the American University of Beirut and is currently pursuing an MA degree in Creative Writing at the University of West Anglia. *The One-eyed Man* was originally written for an advanced Creative Writing seminar.

MISHKA MOJABBER MOURANI started writing at the onset of the Lebanese war in 1975. Although she was born in Egypt, her parents are Greek and Lebanese. Mourani has worked as an educational consultant in the Middle East and Africa as well as an external reviewer and publishing consultant for a number of American and British publishers. She is the author of a series of textbooks and a poetry collection, *Lest We Forget 1975–1990, written* during the war years. Currently she is Senior Vice President of the International College in Beirut.

EVELYN SHAKIR, the daughter of Lebanese immigrants, is the author of *Bint Arab: Arab and Arab American Women in the United States* (Praeger,1997). Her short stories have appeared in *Post Gibran: An Anthology of New Arab American Writing*, the *Red Cedar Reviews*, *Flyway* and the *Knight Literary Journal*. One of her personal essays was recently published in *Massachusetts Review*, and her essays on Arab-American literature have appeared in a number of journals and collections. Shakir has written and produced a radio documentary on Syrians and Lebanese in the Boston area. In 1999 she spent a semester as a Fulbright Fellow in Lebanon.

EMILY NASRALLAH was born in 1931 and raised in the small southern Lebanese village of al-Kfayr at the foot of Mount Hermon. She was educated at the Beirut College for Women and the American University of Beirut. Nasrallah, who has been writing for thirty-six years, is the acclaimed author of six novels, four children's books, six collections of short stories and a six-volume biographical series about pioneer women from the East and West. Her first book, *Tuyur Aylul (September Birds,*1962) won two prizes and in 1991 she was given the Khalil Jibran award in literature.

NADA RAMADAN graduated with an MA in French Literature from the Lebanese University. She contributes regular reviews and essays to a number of Lebanese newspapers including *an-Nahar*. Her work explores social and domestic issues that focus primarily on the lives of women.

HANAN AL-SHAYKH was born and brought up in Lebanon. After pursuing a successful career in journalism, writing for *an-Nahar*, she moved to London where she now lives with her family. Al-Shaykh is the acclaimed author of seven acclaimed novels including *The Story of Zahra*, *Women of Sand and Myrrh*, two volumes of short stories and two plays. Her latest book, *Hikayati Sharhun Yatul*, is about her mother.

ALAWIYA SOBH is a writer, novelist and journalist. Her story collection, *Slumber*, was published in 1986; *Stories by Mariam* in 2002; and her latest novel, *Dunia,* in 2005. Since 1990 Sobh has edited a magazine that focuses on issues related to women and family life. During the war she wrote a series of radio programmes which gained instant popularity.

NADINE R. L. TOUMA, an artist and writer, was inspired by the high incidence of plastic surgery in Beirut (in her own words, 'western noses on eastern faces') to make 6,000 marzipan noses that she sold from a vegetable truck on the city's streets. Her installation 'Haremharrasment: Cairo St Courtship', was first shown in the 2003 exhibition *Harem Fantasies and the New Scheherazades* in the Center de Cultura Contemporania de Barcelona before going on tour in Europe. Touma's film "She Comes From a Good Family" was featured in the 2003 International Exhibitionist art series, a short season of art films in London and her latest work, *Sayyidi Milady,* is a collection of poems and letters. Recently she has created a publishing house for children's books written in Arabic.

PATRICIA SARRAFIAN WARD was born and brought up in Beirut, Lebanon, and holds an MFA from the University of Michigan, where she received Hopwood Awards in Novel and Short Fiction. Her writing has appeared in several journals, most recently a short story in the anthology *Dinarzad's Children* and a satirical cartoon in *Mizna*. Her novel *The Bullet Collection* (Graywolf Press, 2003) received the GLCA New Writers Award, the Anahid Literary Award and the Hala Maksoud Award for Outstanding Emerging Writer. She currently lives on Sandy Hook Bay, New Jersey.

NAZIK SABA YARED was Professor of Arabic Literature at the Lebanese American University until 1998. Educated at the American University of Beirut (PhD, 1976), she has subsequently published fifteen books (fiction and non-fiction) as well as stories for young people. Among her recent publications are *Cancelled Memories* (1998); *Arab Travelers and the West* (1991); *Improvisations on a Missing String* (1992); and *Secularism and the Arab World* (2002). Yared has received several awards, including one from the Lebanese Association for Children's Books (1997), the Prince Claus Award (1998), and the *Chevalier dans l'Ordre des Palmes Académiques* (1997).

IMAN HUMAYDAN YOUNES graduated with a BA from the

American University of Beirut and is currently working on an MA in sociology. Her first novel *B for a House Named Beirut* (1997) was followed by *Tut Barri* (Wild Mulberries). Many of her short stories and articles have appeared in Arabic newspapers and magazines.